Diary of a 6th Grade
NINJA

My Worst
Frenemy

Diary of a 6th Grade
NINJA

BOOK 10
My Worst Frenemy

MARCUS EMERSON

ILLUSTRATED BY **DAVID LEE**

ALLEN&UNWIN
SYDNEY·MELBOURNE·AUCKLAND·LONDON

First published by Allen & Unwin in 2017

Allen & Unwin
83 Alexander Street
Crows Nest NSW 2065
Australia
Phone: (61 2) 8425 0100
Email: info@allenandunwin.com
Web: www.allenandunwin.com

A Cataloguing-in-Publication entry is available
from the National Library of Australia
www.trove.nla.gov.au

ISBN 978 1 76029 564 6

Cover design by Marcus Emerson and Sandra Nobes
Text design by Sandra Nobes
Cover and internal illustrations by David Lee
Set in 14 pt Adobe Garamond by Sandra Nobes
Printed and bound in Australia by Griffin Press

5 7 9 10 8 6 4

www.marcusemerson.com

This one's for Hazel...

Here's a bit of advice for anyone out there who'd like to be a villain someday – if your phone rings, *answer* it. What's the point in making evil demands if you're just gonna *ignore* phone calls?

That's what Vesh was doing... and that's why Naoki and I were scaling a building using nothing but thin rope. You ever climb a building with a thin rope? I don't recommend it.

Wait.

Let me start again so things make more sense.

Naoki and I were walking up the side of a hundred-storey building. At the top was one of the most notorious criminals our galaxy had ever seen. We weren't sure whether he was expecting us or not, but I guess we were about to find out.

Vesh had taken the Earth hostage, threatening to use his ultra powerful planet-eating machine on the planet unless he was paid a quadrillion fossil credits. You know how many zeroes are in a quadrillion?

Fifteen. That's 1,000,000,000,000,000.

I guess it's a good thing he didn't ask for *two* quadrillion fossil credits, right?

The people of Earth tried to contact Vesh several times in the hope of working out a deal that didn't end with the destruction of the planet, because, y'know … that kind of thing really ruins your day.

But Vesh never answered a single phone call.

I know, right? What kind of alien monster carries around a clunky phone to begin with? Bad guys need better tech than that. Total noob.

And Vesh was *clearly* ignoring the calls. It would ring twice, and then go straight to voicemail. That dude was clicking the ignore button … but why?

Oh, and the text messages us Earthlings sent to him were delivered – Vesh still had read receipts on, so we could see that he got the messages.

C'mon, Vesh! *Be a better villain!*

So... that's when yours truly was called upon to save the day. Again.

My name is Chase Cooper, and I'm a sixth grade ninja... scaling a building to meet with an alien who refuses to answer his phone.

Naoki, my trusty raccoon sidekick, was ahead of me, clawing his way up the side of the building. His backpack was slung over his shoulder and dangled above my face.

'You mind strapping your bag tighter?' I said, as his bag brushed the tip of my nose.

'Sorry, master,' Naoki said. 'If I had an extra paw right now, I'd totally do it, but I fear I might fall.'

'Right,' I said. 'Just concentrate on climbing.'

'If Vesh would've just answered his stinkin' phone, we wouldn't have to do any of this!' Naoki said. 'And his demands for fossil credits!

If he'd answered his phone, he'd know nobody has a clue what a fossil credit is! Are they even real? It's like demanding a bajillion unicorn horns!'

I laughed at his frustration. Naoki's mouth ran like a river when he was upset.

'Dude,' I said. 'It'll all work out in the end. All we have to do is get to the top of the building and talk some sense into an evil alien who wants to destroy the planet. Too easy.'

A loudspeaker crackled from somewhere in the sky.

'Attention, citizens of Earth,' said a deep, dark, kind of reptilian voice. 'Due to your failure to pay me, your planet will be devoured in just a few short minutes ...'

'We must hurry, master!' Naoki said, taking larger steps against the side of the building.

I clutched the rope tighter, pulling myself up as fast as I could.

Suddenly one of the windows on the side of the building slid open. I flinched, thinking Vesh had sent down a bunch of spiders or something to stop me from getting to him. And when I saw who opened the window, I *wished* it were a bunch of spiders.

It was Wyatt, and he had a determined, I'm-here-to-help look in his eye.

'Sup, guys?' Wyatt said, leaning out the window. 'Whatcha doin' out here?'

Naoki groaned. 'What's it look like? *We're tryin' to save the world!*'

'Yeah,' I said. 'Little busy right now.'

'It's cool,' Wyatt said, scooting across the windowsill and grabbing the rope. 'I'll help!'

'No, no,' I said. The rope tightened as Wyatt hopped from the window and hung below me. 'We're good, man! We don't need any help!'

'Yes you do!' Wyatt said. 'Be like water, bro!'

'*What?*' I said.

'He said "be like water",' Naoki said through clenched teeth. 'Water flows, transforms, adapts to its surroundings, no matter what they are.'

'You got it,' Wyatt said. 'I'm here and I'm helping. *Deal with it!*'

'Master,' Naoki whispered. 'We don't have time to argue with him. Vesh is only *minutes* away from destroying the world!'

I looked down to tell Wyatt that if he wanted to help, he had to be careful. But I didn't get a chance to get the words out.

Wyatt grabbed the bottom of my jeans and pulled himself up. He climbed up my back.

'So how'd you guys get this gig?' Wyatt asked as he rudely planted his feet on my shoulders to boost himself higher. 'Do you freelance your ninja services or something?'

'Freelance?' Naoki repeated.

'Yeah, like, working for yourself, finding jobs to pay the bills,' Wyatt explained. 'So, like, do you two go around finding random jobs like this and getting paid for your trouble?'

'Random jobs,' Naoki whispered sarcastically. 'Like saving the planet from total destruction...'

'Of course not!' I said. 'There's no pay cheque! We're doing this because our *planet* is being threatened by an alien monster!'

'Huh,' Wyatt grunted, unimpressed. 'Then you guys are bad at business, which is good for me. I don't have a ninja clan anymore, so I'm looking to branch out on my own, y'know? I'm gonna do what you're doing, but *better* and for a fee.'

Wyatt grabbed Naoki's tail and swung back and forth.

'Let go of my tail or feel the wrath of my ancestors!' Naoki growled.

'Look at me, guys!' Wyatt squealed, swinging by Naoki's furry tail. 'I'm a monkey!'

'Wyatt!' I said, feeling like a frustrated parent. 'Let go of his tail this instant! We're gonna fall if you don't stop acting like a little kid!'

Planting both feet on the side of the building, Wyatt stopped swinging. He pulled himself up over Naoki so he was at the front. And then he stuck out his tongue and blew a raspberry at me.

'Seriously?' I yelled.

From the top of the building, a silver robotic eye peeked over the edge and spotted us. It must've been one of Vesh's cameras because it suddenly flashed red, and an alarm thundered through the entire building.

'Great,' I said. 'So much for our surprise attack.'

Naoki gasped. 'Master, look out! Tiny ninja robots are falling from the rooftop!'

'Tiny ninja robots?' Wyatt said. 'Flippin' sweet!'

The ninjas fell around us like rain. Several of them landed on our shoulders and attacked. You'd think tiny robot ninjas attacking you would kind of tickle, but I'm here to tell you it *doesn't* tickle ... it hurts.

Wyatt's attitude quickly shifted from delight to terror.

'Get 'em off me!' Wyatt screeched. 'They're punching me with their tiny fists!'

'They're punching *all* of us with their tiny fists!' Naoki said.

Flailing wildly, Wyatt did the dumbest thing a person can do while climbing a building with a thin rope – he let go.

Naoki shouted as Wyatt fell on top of him. Naoki was a strong raccoon, but when someone three times your size slams into you

from above, it doesn't matter how tightly you're holding on – you're gonna fall.

And then there was me at the bottom, staring helplessly as they came crashing down on top of me.

The rope burned my hands as I slid down. I let go and arched myself back, reaching out for the nearest windowsill, but they were all too far away. Naoki, Wyatt and I fell into a freefall.

The air was brisk and bit my cheeks through my ninja mask as I fell faster and faster, spinning uncontrollably. The tiny robot ninjas flaked off my shoulders, probably heading back to Vesh, who was still on the roof.

Was that it? Was that the way the world was going to end? What were the history books going to say about it, I wondered. Then I realised there wouldn't *be* any history books written about it ... ever.

Wyatt was hollering from somewhere I couldn't see. He sounded like he was having fun!

And then there came another sound, like an explosion. It was close – a little *too* close.

Something grabbed the bottom of my jeans and stopped me from spinning like a violent ballerina. It was Naoki!

'Hang on, master!' Naoki shouted as he tightened his grip on me. In his hand was Wyatt.

On Naoki's back was a jetpack, blasting fire. Oh my god, his backpack was a jetpack!

Wait ... his backpack was a jetpack??

'*You have a jetpack?*' I shouted over the noise of the rockets. 'Why didn't you use that thing to begin with? We could've skipped the whole "climbing the side of the building with cheap rope" thing!'

'I never said anything because you never asked, master!' Naoki replied.

'Okay, from now on, tell me if you have a tool that'll help *any* of our missions!'

Naoki smiled. 'Understood!'

The three of us rocketed to the top of the building, where Vesh was working on his planet-eating machine. He was hunched over the foot of the machine as sparks danced around him.

Naoki gently dropped Wyatt and me on the roof, and landed between us.

Vesh stopped his work on the machine, and stood. The alien was at least three metres tall. He was still wearing his space helmet.

He arched his back, stretching like he had just come home from a long day at work. Slowly, like creepy-horror-movie slow, he turned around to face us.

That's when I realised his body wasn't what I thought it was. It was just a robotic shell that was controlled by a tiny little alien sitting inside the helmet on top.

Vesh was an itty-bitty little thing. If he weren't about to destroy the world, I would've said he was kind of cute. He was even wearing a tiny t-shirt!

The alien clapped his hands slowly, like he was applauding. 'Well, well, well,' he said from inside the glass helmet. 'If it isn't Charley Cooper.'

'It's *Chase*,' I said, correcting him. 'My name's Chase, dude.'

'Charley, Chase, it doesn't make a lick of difference, does it?' Vesh said, holding one of his hands out, presenting the machine that was behind him. 'In a few short minutes, your planet will be *toast*, and *nobody* will remember you.'

'Why haven't you answered your phone?' Naoki huffed.

Vesh shrugged his tiny shoulders. 'I prefer texting.'

'We *did* text you!' Naoki added.

'I'm not too good with new technology.' He held his gigantic robot hands in front of his face. 'I've got these fat fingers and phone buttons are super tiny.'

'So that's why our planet is going to be destroyed?' Wyatt replied. *'Because of your giant sausage fingers?'*

'Dude, easy,' Naoki said.

'Oh, I'm sorry,' Wyatt said sarcastically. 'We

wouldn't want to hurt his feelings, right?'

'He wants to blow up the planet,' I said. 'You gotta be more careful when you—'

Wyatt leaned his head back and groaned. 'You buncha dandelions! Watch how a *pro* does this,' he said, marching towards Vesh.

'What're you doing?' I whispered harshly. 'I've got this under control!'

Wyatt spun around with his arms outstretched. 'Really? This is "under control" to you?'

'I mean,' I stammered, 'I was *about* to talk him out of it!'

'You were going to *negotiate*?' Wyatt said. 'Forget that! I negotiate with my *fists*!'

With that, Wyatt turned and sprinted straight for the three-metre-tall robot shell that contained Vesh.

Wyatt flipped over, somehow changing into his red ninja robes. Honestly, if the planet weren't in danger of being eaten, I would've thought his stunt was pretty cool.

Vesh planted one foot behind him. At first, it

looked like he was bracing himself for Wyatt's attack, but it quickly became clear that he didn't care about Wyatt. Instead, he set his hands on the planet-eating machine and brought up a holographic control panel.

Screeching, Wyatt flew through the air, throwing out a kick that would crack any kung fu master up. It looked like Wyatt was riding an invisible bicycle.

'What move is that?' Naoki asked.

'It's not in any book *I've* ever read,' I said.

Sadly, Wyatt's move failed on a level so epic that even *I* felt embarrassed for him. His bicycle kick landed directly on Vesh's back, but... have you ever hit a tiny rock while skateboarding? It doesn't matter how fast you're going, once your wheel hits that rock, you fall flat to the ground like a ragdoll. You could be coasting at a hundred kilometres an hour, and then *BAM!* You face plant into the ground so hard that people on the other side of the world cringe.

Wyatt hit the ground and screamed in pain.

Vesh didn't even flinch. He was focused on the holographic display in front of him, twisting and turning dials until he finally found what he was looking for.

The alien put his hand directly into the middle of a blue holographic sphere, clenched his fist and turned his wrist.

The planet-eating machine came to life. The sound was so loud that I couldn't hear anything but the grinding noise it made.

Naoki covered his ears and shouted, but I had to read his lips in order to understand him.

'You have to stop the machine! We have to switch it off!' he said.

'But how? I don't know anything about that thing, do you?' I mouthed back.

Naoki shook his head.

I looked at the city streets below us. The planet-eating machine was already working cracking open the ground. Cars and buses had lifted off the ground and were being thrown back and forth like toys.

Naoki tugged at my jeans, pointing back at

Vesh's machine. There, on the side of the monstrous machine, was a plug hooked up to a socket on the rooftop. 'For real?' I said.

I ran for the plug. Vesh turned towards me, but I was too quick for him. I grabbed the thick wire around the plug and yanked as hard as I could. Lucky for me, and the rest of the planet, the plug slipped out.

The cars bouncing around on the city streets crashed to the concrete as gravity returned to normal.

'You fool!' Vesh screamed from his glass helmet. 'You're only delaying the inevitable! I'll return to your pathetic planet and finish the job later!'

'Not if I stop you first!' I shouted. My ears were ringing from the noise Vesh's machine made…was *still* making.

Vesh's machine was still surging with power!

Vesh pointed at the ground under his feet. A burst of green light shot out from his fingertip, creating a swirling portal.

'How can you stop me when you're too busy

saving yourself?' Vesh growled. And then he stepped through the portal and disappeared.

'The machine!' Naoki shouted. 'It's gonna blow!'

The rooftop shook violently. Little pebbles danced around our feet.

'We have to switch it off!' I said.

'But you *unplugged* it!' Naoki said. 'What else can we do?'

I looked at the plug. The gears glowed red as flames shot from the top of the device.

'Nothing is ever as easy as it seems!' Wyatt shouted from behind.

I spun around in time to see Wyatt yank Naoki's jetpack off his tiny raccoon body. Every muscle in my body burned as I ran after him.

'Wait!' I said as Wyatt pulled the jetpack over his arms. 'That thing can carry all three of us! We can *all* escape if you just wait!'

Wyatt leapt from the roof, spinning to face me. 'Too late, losers!'

My feet dug into the ground, and I slid to a stop inches away from the edge. The little pebbles at my feet slipped over the side and fell to the street below, which, by the way, was about a hundred floors down.

Naoki's voice came from behind me. 'Jump!'

As I turned around, Naoki leapt towards my chest, pushing me over the edge. Vesh's machine exploded, rattling the entire building. Glass windows shattered from the force.

The heat from the blast was so intense that I could feel the warmth even as Naoki and I were falling down the side of the building.

Air screamed past my ears as I tried to steady myself. We were only seconds away from hitting the ground. I had to think of something quick.

And then I heard Wyatt's laughter. He was floating in place high in the sky, watching Naoki and me fall.

Naoki gripped my head and shook it. 'Pay attention, man! You gotta think of something!'

I stuttered, but I don't know what I said. It was like my brain was totally wiped clean. I opened my mouth to talk, but the only thing that came out was a scream.

 Monday.
My locker.

'Whooooa, Chase!' Brayden said like I was a horse he was trying to stop.

I was on the floor in front of my locker, coughing from the scream I had just let out. I could hear kids laughing at me.

There, standing in front of me, was my cousin Zoe and my best friend Brayden.

Brayden looked embarrassed for me, keeping his eyes turned to the ground. Zoe held her hands to her chest as if she had just been frightened.

'Dude, what's the matter with you?' Zoe said.

I froze, waiting for Vesh to burst through the crowd.

'This is it, isn't it?' Zoe asked. 'You've finally snapped. When I tell my kids about their zany Uncle Chase, I'll start with this *exact* moment. "He lost it in the middle of school," I'll say. "He had no way to control the volume of his voice ... always screaming instead of talking."'

I swallowed hard, looking around.

Other students whispered loud enough that I could hear them.

'*What a weirdo.*'

'*He should've stayed at his old school.*'

'*He's been nothing but trouble since he got here.*'

My face felt warm, and I had a sick feeling in my stomach.

'Am I still dreaming?' I asked as I pushed against my locker to help me stand.

'Ah,' Zoe said. 'Nightmares in the middle of school?'

I wiped the sleep from my eyes and pulled my cheeks down to stretch my face. I was still groggy. 'I mean, is this real life?'

'What if this is a dream *inside* a dream?' Brayden said. 'Do you know what *that* would mean?'

'No,' I said. 'What would it mean?'

Brayden shrugged and shook his head. 'Oh, I don't know. That's why I asked.'

I've known Brayden since the first week of school. We've had our rough patches, but every friendship does. My dad says it's what turns 'kind of friends' into 'best friends'. I'm not gonna argue with my dad. He seems to know what he's talking about ... *most* of the time.

I felt a sting on my forearm. Zoe's fingers were pinched around the skin above my wrist.

'Ouch!' I yelped, pulling away.

'You're supposed to pinch *yourself* to wake up,' Brayden said to Zoe.

'Yeah!' I said, rubbing my arm. 'I was supposed to pinch *myself!*'

Zoe pinched a spot on my other arm.

'*Stop that!*' I yelped.

Zoe smiled. 'Well, you're not dreaming anymore.'

I folded my arms, rubbing both spots Zoe had pinched. I couldn't pinch anyone like that if I practised it a thousand times. What is it about girls just *knowing* how to inflict *that* much pain with only two fingers?

Brayden unzipped his book bag and took out a small black glass bottle, about the size of a trading card. He popped off the cap, held it to his neck, and sprayed it onto his skin.

'Cologne, huh?' I said. 'Dude perfume.'

25

'Hey, dude,' Brayden said slyly, posing like he was in a magazine ad. 'Ladies dig it when you smell like a man.'

'You smell like a pine tree,' Zoe said, waving her hands to keep the cologne from wafting over to her. 'And your pine-tree mist is all over my shirt! Now *I* smell like a man!'

'Sorry,' Brayden said, pushing the cap back onto his cologne bottle. 'I forgot to spray it on before I left home.'

'So your only other option was to do it in a packed hallway?' Zoe said, annoyed. 'You should've gone to the locker room!'

'I did!' Brayden said. 'I sprayed it there first … and now I'm spraying here.'

Zoe dropped her arms, shocked. '*Once. Once* is enough!'

'Okaaaay,' Brayden said, raising his eyebrows and bobbing his head back and forth.

I glanced up and down the hallway, watching all the other students walk with their friends.

'Why were you napping in front of your locker?' Zoe asked.

'I was waiting for Naomi,' I said. 'We're going to go to the assembly in the library together.'

Naomi was another one of my best friends. Brayden and I had our rough patches, but Naomi and I were trying to rebuild some seriously burnt bridges.

I won't go into detail, because there's *a lot* of detail, but basically – she betrayed me, pretended to be my friend, tried to destroy my life, came back and apologised, and then sacrificed her own social life to make it up to me. So, yeah … there's a lot of history between us.

'If she was supposed to meet you at your locker,' Zoe said, 'where is she?'

'Maybe she got caught in a hall jam,' I said.

'Maybe she's plotting to destroy you,' Zoe said, but closed her eyes and shook her head as soon as she said it. 'No, no, no. I didn't mean that. It's just … she hasn't showed up. You sure you can trust her? Not that I'm saying you shouldn't, but y'know … just asking.'

Even though Naomi and I were talking again, Zoe had a point. And it had crossed my mind since Naomi apologised.

I nodded. 'I trust her,' I said. 'But can we really be sure we can trust anybody?'

'Um, yeah,' Zoe said. 'I'm pretty sure I know who I can and can't trust.'

Brayden straightened his posture and spoke in a much deeper voice than normal. 'Forgiveness is what makes good men great.'

'Stop trying to be a man,' Zoe sighed.

Brayden smiled. 'All I'm sayin' is that it's a good thing Naomi and Chase are friends again.'

'She said sorry, and I believe she is,' I said. 'Isn't that the only thing that matters?'

'It is,' Zoe said. 'Normally, I'm the one who makes all the mature decisions. It's nice to see you do that for a change.'

I gave Zoe the dorkiest smile I could.

She laughed. 'Nerd.'

'But…' I said, scanning the crowd one last time, 'I don't think she's coming.'

'Maybe she got caught up,' Brayden said.

I sighed. 'Maybe.'

Brayden, Zoe and I made our way through the halls, to the library for the assembly.

This is probably a good time to fill you in on all the stuff that's happened so far.

It's only been a few days since the whole thing with Victor went down in the cafeteria.

Victor planned the whole shebang. He was an eighth grader who wore an earring and dressed like he was in a boy band – y'know, two collared shirts, both flipped up, along with baggy pants that looked like something my parents used to wear in high school. He had glasses too, but I doubted they were even real.

He was also the leader of the Scavengers, a group of kids who know the secrets of everyone in the school. They eavesdrop on your conversation, read your text messages over your shoulder, and steal all the notes you wrote to your friends right out of the bin. The Scavengers know everything. Those tiny little secrets you think you're keeping safe in your head? The Scavengers know.

And Victor had planned to use that power to ruin my life, but thanks to Naomi, he didn't get away with it.

The last time I saw Victor, a couple of hall monitors in suits and sunglasses were escorting him out of the cafeteria. It was kind of weird … like he was being taken away by secret agents or something.

The Scavengers hadn't said a word to me since, but that didn't mean they weren't around. I'd bet my whole comic book collection that I haven't seen the last of them.

Well, not my *whole* comic book collection. The variant-cover editions are comin' with me to my grave.

Oh, and on top of dealing with the Scavengers, there was also some trouble with the red ninjas *and* a group of new *green* ninjas.

Wyatt (remember him from my dream?) is the leader of the red ninja clan … well, he *used* to be their leader. His ninja clan grew so big

Diary of a 6th Grade NINJA

Scavengers + Victor = Horrible

Wyatt − Red ninjas = Less Horrible

Red ninjas + Green ninjas = Holiday Ninjas?

that he couldn't control them anymore, and they sort of kicked him out. The red ninjas probably have a new leader now, but I have no idea who it is.

It was the same with the green ninja clan that recently sprouted up. They're kind of the mystery of the week.

And me? I'm just trying to coast through the

31

rest of the school year. Dealing with the Scavengers, Victor, Wyatt, and different ninja clans is more than any sixth grader needs on their plate.

At this point, 'cool' isn't something I want anymore. I've been hated by so many different people the past couple of months that honestly, one step above where I'm at would make me happy.

I just don't want to be hated anymore.

 **Monday.
The lobby.**

I turned the corner and stopped outside the lobby. Brayden and Zoe were still with me, and everyone was waiting to get into the library.

'Zoe, you're the president,' I said. 'Why don't you just push your way through the crowd?'

'Doesn't work like that,' Zoe said.

'Oh, right,' Brayden said. 'You're supposed to have bodyguards and stuff do that for you.'

Zoe laughed. 'I wish! I wouldn't mind a crew walking me everywhere.'

My eyebrows raised. 'Hey, you've got Brayden and me! We're all the crew you need!'

'My own ninja bodyguards,' Zoe said quietly, and then paused. 'That's not such a bad idea, but I think I'd come off as more of a villain if I travelled with ninjas everywhere I went.'

'If by "villain", you mean "way cool president",' I said, 'then yes, you'd be a way cool president.'

Zoe sighed, standing up on her tiptoes to see over everyone's head. 'C'mon, man. This is taking forever. The crowd's barely moving. Are the doors even open?'

I tried to see past everyone, but the crowd was too thick.

'I dunno,' I said. 'At least everyone's excited to get in there.'

'They should be,' Zoe said, dropping back to her heels. 'It wasn't easy to get Dr Tenderfoot to visit. He doesn't really do school visits.'

'Tenderfoot,' I said. 'Who's this guy again?'

'Dr Ashley Tenderfoot,' Zoe said. She was going to continue, but Brayden cut her off.

'Dude's name is Ashley?' Brayden said, scrunching his nose. 'That's a girl's name.'

'Um, no, it's not,' Zoe said, crossing her arms.

'And you better not say anything about it when we're in there. Dr Tenderfoot is a highly respected pioneer in robotics research. He founded Tenderfoot Industries.'

TENDERFOOT
INDUSTRIES

I leaned closer to Brayden and whispered, 'That means he's supes important.'

'He's not *just* supes important,' Zoe said. 'He's, like, *the* dude everyone talks about when they talk about robotics. His lab is working on some pretty amazing stuff.'

'Like end-of-the-world amazing?' I said. 'Is he going to build the machines that turn against humans someday?'

'Maybe,' Zoe said. 'But for now, we're probably safe.'

The doors to the library must've opened because the crowd shuffled forward like zombies in search of their next meal.

'It took a *ton* of emails to get Dr Tenderfoot to agree to come here for the week,' Zoe continued. 'And he only did it because we agreed to host a robotics competition for the students.'

'Ooooooh!' I said, excited. 'Like, getting robots to fight each other in the ring?'

'No,' Zoe replied. 'Like, getting a couple of teams of students to build their own robot.'

'And then getting them to fight to the death? Their *robot* death?' Brayden said.

'Oh my god, no,' Zoe said. 'The teams will build their own robot and then, at the end of the week, present them to the school and Dr Tenderfoot. Best one wins.'

'Wins what?' I asked, crossing my fingers for a robot sidekick.

'A robot sidekick,' Zoe said.

My jaw dropped.

'I know you too well,' Zoe laughed. 'I don't know what the prize is, but I can guarantee you it's not that.'

'Oh,' I said, kicking a spot on the carpet like a little child. 'Robot sidekicks are cool,' I whispered.

'So wait,' Brayden said as we shuffled forwards. 'They expect a bunch of sixth graders to *build* a robot? Like it's that easy?'

'No,' Zoe said, shaking her head. 'Just wait until you get in there. Dr Tenderfoot will explain the whole thing better than I can.'

We finally reached the library. The room was packed, with most of the kids standing since there weren't any seats left.

Suddenly, a creepy, dark voice came from behind us. 'Mistah Coooooopah!'

I recognised the voice immediately. It was Naomi.

'Sup, dude?' Naomi said, nudging me with her shoulder.

'Hey!' I said, happy to see her.

'You weren't at your locker,' Naomi said.

'Oh, but he was,' Zoe sighed, making it obvious that she wasn't happy that Naomi and I were friends again. I knew Zoe didn't want to see me get burned again.

'You were?' Naomi said.

'I sorta fell asleep,' I mumbled

'Dude,' Naomi said. 'You gotta lay off the late-night video games.'

'Okay,' I said, 'but we were playing online *together*.'

Naomi tried to hide a smile but couldn't.

Zoe rolled her eyes the way an adult would wag their finger.

'We'll be inside,' Zoe said, grabbing Brayden's elbow.

'Wait,' Brayden said. 'I don't wanna go in yet. I'll go in when Chase does.'

Zoe gave him a quick look. Brayden sighed and followed her into the library.

'Finally,' Naomi said. 'Now that we're alone…my Scavengers will *crush* you for good!'

Oh, great. Maybe Zoe was right about Naomi after all.

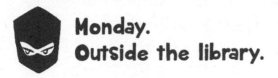

Monday.
Outside the library.

'Uh … okay?' I said.

Naomi laughed and threw her arms around me. 'I'm kidding!'

Naomi squeezed me so hard that my throat let out a weird squawk.

'Did you just quack at me?' Naomi asked.

'Maybe,' I said, embarrassed.

'You know I was joking, right?' Naomi said. 'Too soon?'

I chuckled, feeling relieved. 'No, it's cool. I was just a little shocked.'

'I know,' Naomi said. 'You were so shocked you *quacked*.'

Pushing open the door to the library, I let Naomi go in first.

Once Naomi walked past, I tucked my thumbs into my armpits and started flapping my elbows and quacking loudly.

'*Quack, quack!*' I said, marching through door. '*Quack, quack, qua—*'

'Have you quite finished?' a man asked me in a stern voice.

The library was dead quiet, except for a few giggles here and there. In the middle of the library was a man with a moustache, a top hat, and a microphone. He was halfway up the staircase that went up to the second floor. He looked like something from a steampunk comic book – like an old-fashioned professor who builds time machines out of train parts.

'Uhh…' I stammered. My brain was busy packing its bags because it had given up on me. 'Sorry.'

A cricket chirped somewhere in the room. It was probably laughing at me too.

The moustached man spoke awkwardly into

the microphone. 'We'll wait until you're seated.'

It was the longest walk I'd ever experienced. Everyone in the library watched as I weaved through the crowd. The library was completely silent, so every time my book bag scraped across someone's clothing, it felt like it was screaming for everyone to gawk at me.

'Sorry 'bout that,' I said, bumping into a bunch of kids. 'Excuse me. Um, I'm sorry. *Sorrrrry!* Your book bag is blocking my— *thaaaanks*. Sorry!'

Finally, after what felt like a thousand hours, I found my friends sitting at one of the desks in the middle of the library. Zoe and Brayden were sitting next to each other, and Gidget and Slug were across from them.

My ninja clan was down to three members besides me – Gidget, Slug and Brayden. After months of trying to keep my ninja clan large, it was a relief to have a small, loyal team. Faith was also sitting with them, next to an empty seat.

Faith, for those keeping track, had a secret of her own. I'd found myself in more than a few sticky situations this year, and Faith had been there to bail me out each time...but it *wasn't* as Faith. It was as the *white ninja*.

She knew I knew, but every time I brought it up, she changed the subject. She was up to something. I just didn't know what yet. All I

knew was that she was on my side, and that was all that mattered.

Naomi was in front of me, pulling out the empty seat next to Faith.

Faith smiled at Naomi. 'Sorry, this seat is for Chase.'

My gut twisted because I knew my friends still didn't trust Naomi.

'It's cool,' I whispered. 'She can have it.'

'Young man, another interruption from you, and I'll have to dole out a consequence,' the man at the microphone said.

I leaned towards Zoe. 'Can he do that?'

'Chase, this guy can do whatever he wants, so *stop* talking!'

A low chuckle came from the speakers. 'It's alright, Zoe,' the man said. 'Apparently your friend hasn't a clue who I am, so allow me to introduce myself... well, *reintroduce* myself since you were absent when I did it the first time.'

Kids in the library made an '*Ohhhhhhhh*' sound.

'My name,' the man with the moustache said, pausing for effect, 'is Dr Ashley Tenderfoot.'

'Oh, man,' I whispered. The man was wearing a top hat and a tuxedo jacket, along with a pair of blue jeans and sneakers. And over his right eye was a monocle.

I never understood monocles. It was like someone said, 'I need glasses, but only for half the number of eyes I have.'

'I own and operate Tenderfoot Industries,' Dr

Tenderfoot said. 'Many of you are probably familiar with the work we've done, from hoverbikes to spaceship prototypes. And we're leading the way in state-of-the-art robotics research. We've broken a lot of new ground already, but we've barely scraped the surface!'

Zoe nudged me with her elbow. 'See? This dude's awesome.'

Tenderfoot walked across the staircase platform. 'Your president, Zoe Cooper, and Principal Davis invited me to come and speak to you today, which is something I *never* do. However,' Tenderfoot paused, 'there was something *different* about this invitation. I couldn't put my finger on it, but something told me I *had* to come and see this school for myself.'

Tenderfoot paused again, tapping his finger on the railing of the staircase. He was looking right at me.

He blinked, turning his attention to the other students in the library. 'Zoe and Principal Davis really wanted to "wow" you, and show you that there's a whole world of undiscovered territory in the technological arena.'

Taking a step up the staircase, Tenderfoot wrapped the microphone cord around his wrist.

'Some of the best tech that will exist a hundred years from now hasn't even been *thought* of yet,' he said. 'Think of the craziest science fiction movie you've ever seen ... Now imagine you live in that world. Massive spaceships, so large that you can see their silhouettes against the clear blue sky. A weekend trip to see the rings of Saturn. An *actual* journey to the centre of the earth!'

'That *would* be sweet,' Brayden whispered from across the table.

Tenderfoot's moustache lifted to one side. I think he was smiling. 'Just between us, we've got our best minds working on a little gadget that will allow *squids* to communicate with humans.'

'No way,' Slug said, not even trying to keep his voice down.

Tenderfoot chuckled. 'Yes way!' he said. 'Did

46

you know squids are the most intelligent invertebrates on the planet?' Tenderfoot closed his eyes, nodded, and held out a hand. 'It's controversial, of course, but that doesn't stop our scientists from trying to have a conversation with them... or even challenging them to a video game or two. I can't say too much about it, but I *will* say squids are quite the talkers.'

Brayden leaned into the table again. '*Squid people!* Can you imagine? What if they got so smart they could go to school? Oh, man, what if we had classes with *squids*?'

'Cray craaaaay,' I sang.

Zoe lightly slapped the table. 'They'd get better grades than either of you! Now pay attention!'

Tenderfoot was still talking. '...which is the *real* reason I'm here this week. President Zoe, Principal Davis and I have come up with a little competition for a handful of lucky students. Three teams will be chosen to build a fully functioning robot that—'

Someone from the back of the library shouted, interrupting Dr Tenderfoot. '*Build* a robot? Are you kidding me? Half the kids here don't even know how to make a paper aeroplane!'

Everyone turned to see who had the guts to be so rude. It was Jake, and he was standing with a bunch of his friends, the wolf pack.

Dr Tenderfoot paused, smoothing his moustache with his fingers. His patience was being tested. 'If you had let me finish, you'd know that the robot doesn't have to do anything fancy, and Tenderfoot Industries will supply all the necessary parts. The robot just needs to be able to complete one function, even something as simple as moving from point A to point B. The goal is to *create*, to bring life to something that didn't have life before.'

'Okay,' Jake said, annoyed. 'But that still sounds too complicated for anyone in this room. I mean, c'mon, these kids aren't the freshest eggs in the shop.'

Faith frowned. 'Freshest eggs in the shop?'

Dr Tenderfoot sighed. 'It won't be *quite* as difficult as you're making it sound, but luckily for you, the odds of you being on a team are pretty slim.'

Jake slunk back into the crowd, embarrassed.

'To keep everything simple,' Dr Tenderfoot continued, 'there will only be three teams. The winning team will receive a prize greater than they can even imagine.'

The students in the library murmured with excitement. There's no way I was going to enter, but I still felt queasy at the idea of getting roped into the competition.

'I think it'd be totes sweet to compete,' Zoe whispered. 'But not just anyone can enter. Dr Tenderfoot is going to pick the team leaders out of a hat.'

And just like that, the queasy feeling was gone.

'Nice,' I said. 'I didn't put my name in the hat, so I definitely won't get picked, which is good because I seriously need to recharge my batteries. Just *once*, I'd like to not be in the middle of all the drama.'

Zoe flashed me a devious smile. 'Everyone's name is in the hat. We're *all* entered whether we like it or not.'

I groaned, letting my head fall to the table with a thud. I rolled my head back and forth, until something caught my eye from the skinny window on the door.

As Tenderfoot kept talking, I saw it again – a flash of red and green from the window.

'Holiday ninjas,' I whispered.

'Holiday what?' Zoe asked.

'Um, nothing,' I said. 'Can you watch my stuff for a second?'

'Watch your stuff?' Zoe said quietly. 'What do I do if someone tries to take it? Fight them? Hey, where are you going?'

I didn't bother replying, already weaving back through the crowd. There were red and green ninjas up to something in the halls, and I had to check it out.

Principal Davis was leaning against the wall next to the library doors. He didn't say anything when he saw me – just cocked an eyebrow.

'Uh, I gotta use the bathroom,' I whispered.

The principal sighed as he quietly pushed open the door. I pulled the door closed behind me and it clicked shut.

When I pulled my ninja mask over my face, I heard a boy's voice echo down the halls.

'Seriously?' the boy said. 'I *made* you!'

It was Wyatt...and it sounded like he was in trouble.

'Let's get dangerous,' I whispered.

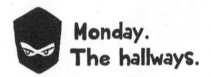

Monday.
The hallways.

I followed Wyatt's voice out of the lobby. I was nervous because Wyatt wasn't even *trying* to keep quiet. It was almost like he *wanted* people to hear him.

About halfway down the hallway, I saw Wyatt pinned against a water fountain that was between two bathrooms.

Two green ninjas stood in front of him doing their best ninja poses.

'I want your names!' Wyatt demanded. 'When this is over, you're *so* out of my ninja clan!'

'We're not even *in* your clan,' one of the ninjas said.

'Just give us your mask,' the other ninja said, 'and we'll let you go. Easy-peasy.'

'There's no way I'm just gonna give you my mask,' Wyatt growled.

My last run-in with the red and green ninjas happened because they were trying to swipe my ninja mask. I only got away from them because I threw my mask down while they were chasing me.

Wyatt had told me that the kid who got my mask would be the leader of the green ninjas.

'Why do you need my mask anyways?' Wyatt said. 'Word is that both the red and green ninja clans have their leaders. Whoever took my red ninjas from me made themselves leader *without* my mask. And that noob, Chase, just let you *have* his mask!'

'Aw, thanks, Wyatt,' I whispered to myself. 'It's not like I'm out here trying to help you.'

The ninja sighed. 'Look, dude, you're washed up. You have no power over the red ninjas anymore, and our new orders are to take your mask anyway. We don't want you pretendin' to be a ninja.'

'*Pretending?*' Wyatt said defensively. 'Without *me*, the red ninjas wouldn't even *exist*!'

'You wanna argue? Take it up with their new leader,' the green ninja said. 'I'm sure he'd *love* to hear from you.'

'I *would* if I knew who he was,' Wyatt said.

'Their new leader?' the ninja asked. 'It's—'

The other green ninja slapped his friend's

shoulder. 'Don't speak his name! That's the
number one rule! And also number two. Like,
the first *ten* rules are that we never say his
name!'

The two green ninjas took a step forwards.
From where I was standing, I could see that
Wyatt's hands were shaking.

Wyatt had been a pain in my neck since the
first day of school, and now I had to decide
whether I should help him or not!

If this were a video game, I would've done
both. I'd save the game right before helping
him and see how it panned out. If it went bad,
I'd just load my save and *not* help him.

But this wasn't a game, and those ninjas
weren't leaving Wyatt alone.

I clenched my jaw because I knew what I
had to do. I never really had a choice anyway.
I decided a long time ago to try to do the right
thing *every* time.

Stepping into the middle of the hallway,
I took a deep breath and shouted, 'Hey, you
guuuuuuuys!'

The two green ninjas turned to look at me.

'Leave him alone!' I said, trying to hide the fear in my voice.

Wyatt glared at me. 'I can handle this!'

I laughed. 'Of course, you're not pinned up against the water fountain or anything, right?'

The two ninjas paused and then relaxed. And I soon found out why. Hands grabbed my arms. I tried to free myself, but there were too many hands on me. Suddenly I was on my back, the ceiling lights close enough to touch. I thought I was hallucinating, until I realised...

They had picked me up.

Wiggling around, I saw that Wyatt was also in the air.

'Give it back!' Wyatt growled.

One of the ninjas was jumping up and down, victoriously waving Wyatt's red ninja mask in the air like a flag. I had managed to pull my own mask off before anyone got hold of it.

'Let go of us!' I said, but obviously the ninjas didn't listen.

Instead, they ran through the halls carrying

me and Wyatt over them. The fluorescent lights zoomed by as the ninjas turned down different hallways.

The ninjas came to a stop right outside the front lobby. I heard the sound of a door click, and then I realised what was about to happen.

The ninjas dumped Wyatt and me through the library doors, where kids were still listening to Dr Tenderfoot's presentation.

Our landing was so rough that both of us shouted in pain. Everyone in the library froze, staring at the two of us.

I was on my stomach. Next to me was Wyatt, his legs digging into my back.

Zoe was glaring at me. The rest of my friends looked shocked.

Principal Davis was hovering above Wyatt and me with the angriest look I'd ever seen on his face.

Principal Davis helped me to my feet. 'This is the second time *today* that you've caused a scene, Chase. And if Dr Tenderfoot hadn't just announced your name, I'd send you to my office.'

'Announced my name?' I asked.

Principal Davis put his hand on Wyatt's shoulder. 'But Dr Tenderfoot didn't say *your* name, so head straight to the front office and wait for me.'

Wyatt didn't argue. He also didn't make eye contact. I thought maybe there were tears in his eyes, but he left the library before I could see.

Principal Davis put his hand on my shoulder and guided me through the crowd as they made a path for me.

'What's going on?' I asked. Principal Davis walked me to the staircase in the middle of the library. Tenderfoot was holding his top hat in his hands. It was upside-down and filled with slips of paper.

Standing next to Tenderfoot were two other kids. One of them I knew well – Wyatt's cousin, Carlyle. The other I only *kinda* knew – Dante.

Carlyle had an ugly habit of talking like a pirate *all the time*. I know, right? *Super* annoying.

'Ah, the quacking child,' Dr Tenderfoot said as he studied me. 'You must be Chase Cooper.'

I smiled tightly because I didn't know what to say.

'Congratulations, Chase Cooper,' Tenderfoot said, waving a small slip of paper. 'You are the team leader of group C, or better yet, Team Cooper.'

I sighed, feeling my stomach drop. 'Greaaaaaat.'

 **Monday.
The library.**

Since Dr Tenderfoot was a special guest speaker,
first period was cancelled. Stations were spread
throughout the library, and there were different
robots at each station – flying drones, tiny
microbots smaller than the tip of a pencil, and
an android-looking thing that freaked me out
every time I looked at it.

I was still standing next to the staircase when
my friends walked up.

'I can't believe you,' Zoe said. 'You *knew* how
important this was to me, and you were in the
hallway goofing off!'

'I wasn't!' I said. 'I was out there because I saw—'

'I don't care if you saw Big Foot out there,' Zoe said. 'You were playing around! You think the only person you affect with your little ninjas hijinks is yourself? It's not! Everyone who laughs at you is also laughing at me, Chase. You're such an embarrassment sometimes!'

Slug raised his eyebrows. 'Ouch.'

Zoe shut her eyes and shook her head. 'I'm sorry,' she sighed. 'It wasn't easy to convince Dr Tenderfoot to come, and I wanted things to be perfect.'

The whole morning was important to my cousin, and I messed it up. *Twice.*

'No,' I said. 'I'm sorry. You're right. I should've stayed at the desk with you guys…'

'What's the deal with you and Wyatt anyway?' Naomi asked. 'What happened?'

I thought about telling everyone about the red and green ninjas, but I didn't. I barely had any info about them so it wasn't the best time.

'It's nothing,' I said. 'I was just goofing off.'

Zoe folded her arms and looked away. 'You're lucky I'm the best cousin ever, or you'd be in the hot seat. Plus, I *have* to forgive you since you're about to ask me to be on your team.'

Scratching the back of my neck, I avoided eye contact. 'Um, I was actually going to find Dr Tenderfoot and ask if I can pass.'

'You're what?' Zoe asked, wide-eyed.

'I've got too much going on,' I said honestly.

Brayden coughed uncomfortably. 'Uh, hey, guys,' he said to the group, 'we should take a look at some of the robots.'

I hoped Zoe would just drop it after everyone left, but she didn't.

'Chase,' she said, 'this is a *huge* opportunity. For both of us! Tenderfoot is going to be remembered for *centuries* because of his inventions! The fact that you've got a chance to sit down and talk to him one on one isn't something that comes along every day!'

'I dunno,' I said, looking for Dr Tenderfoot.

'Seriously, dude,' Zoe said. 'Like, in a hundred years, this place will probably be *filled* with the stuff he's created! People look back and say, "Okay, this is when Dr Tenderfoot changed the world".'

I couldn't see Dr Tenderfoot. His upside-down top hat was still sitting on the other end of the staircase. The slips of paper with the names of students were stuffed inside it, and the three slips he had pulled out were folded neatly and resting next to the hat.

I leaned back, stretching my arm across the steps to grab the folded slips of paper.

'I'm just so drained,' I said to Zoe. 'I'm like a tube of toothpaste that's totally empty but keeps getting squished to get every last drop out.'

'I still think you'd kick yourself later if you didn't at least *try* to work with Dr Tenderfoot,' Zoe said.

I kept quiet but nodded as I played with the slips of paper.

Zoe sat on the step next to me. 'I know you're dealing with a lot right now,' she said. 'And I know that your ninja stuff is all out of whack.'

I looked at Zoe. 'You do?'

Zoe knew about my ninja clan, but I tried to keep most of the drama a secret from her. I didn't want her stressing out over those things.

'C'mon,' she said. 'I'm not an idiot. And Faith and Gidget keep me in the loop.'

'Awesome,' I said sarcastically.

Zoe reached back and pulled Dr Tenderfoot's hat closer. 'He's kind of a weird dude, isn't he?'

'Geniuses can seem odd.'

'Totes. Not in a bad way, but in a way that makes sense. Like, they think differently than everyone else, so they're naturally kinda...weird.'

'I guess.'

'You're impulsive and act without a plan,' Zoe said. 'You do what you want and you don't care what anyone else thinks about you.'

'Um, thanks?' I said.

'I think between the two of us, you're the most like Dr Tenderfoot,' Zoe said. 'You're creative, weird, and totes cray, but you think differently than everyone else. I think you have it in you to win this robotics competition, but I really think you have it in you to become a great man like Dr Tenderfoot.'

Zoe was being super nice, but I still wasn't sure if I wanted to be part of the competition.

And then Zoe's nose scrunched up as she tipped Dr Tenderfoot's hat. Some of the slips of paper fell out.

She scooped them up and dropped them back into the hat. I grabbed a few slips too and shuffled them around on the step next to me.

Zoe looked away, waving to a friend across the room.

I dropped the paper back into Tenderfoot's top hat but noticed something odd. Pushing one of the slips open with my fingers, I saw that it was blank... I opened several other slips and they were blank too.

All the slips of paper in Dr Tenderfoot's hat were *blank*.

The slip of paper that should've had my name on it was blank too.

'What the heck?' I finally said.

'What's up?' Zoe said, looking back at me.

It was one of those moments that last an eternity. I almost showed Zoe the blank slips of paper, but Tenderfoot was her hero. She'd be heartbroken if he was rigging the competition. But maybe he *wasn't* rigging it, and there was a good explanation?

'Nothing,' I said, pushing the slips of paper into Tenderfoot's top hat. And then I pushed it just out of reach. 'I should find Dr Tenderfoot and tell him I'm out of the competition.'

'Ugh,' Zoe said as someone approached us.

'Ahoy, mateys,' said a familiar voice in a terrible pirate accent. 'And where d'ye think yer goin' now?'

It was Carlyle, and he was standing at the bottom of the staircase, blocking our path.

Carlyle was the leader of his own little group of kids who called themselves pirates. They weren't *real* pirates, obvs, but that didn't stop them from dressing and talking like plunderers of the sea.

Carlyle's pirate crew used to be huge, but lately, their club had lost most of its members.

I'm pretty sure it was just Carlyle and a handful of other kids now.

'Carlyle,' I said.

'Cooper,' Carlyle replied, and then looked at Zoe. 'Ahoy, lassie. Good t'see you, as always.'

'Hi,' Zoe said, rolling her eyes.

'What do you want?' I asked.

'I'm here t'size up my competition,' Carlyle said. 'Ya best not try'n hornswoggle the game, mate, or ye'll find yerself in a mess o' trouble ye can't clean.'

I stared. '*What* are you talking about?'

Carlyle smiled. He pointed his finger at me. 'Ye might as well drop out now, Chase! Don't even *bother* tryin' to build a robot 'cause it'll probably end up bein' super lame!'

Something snapped inside me. I felt the sudden need to win this robotics competition.

'Whatever, dude!' I said, stepping down the staircase to get right in his face. 'You know what? I was *going* to drop out of the competition, but now I'm competing just to wipe that smug pirate grin off your face when I win!'

I heard Zoe squeal behind me, excited.

Carlyle narrowed his eyes at me, but said nothing. He clicked his heels together, turned, and marched away.

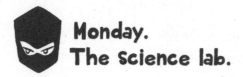 **Monday.
The science lab.**

At the end of the day, my friends and I met in one of the science labs on the second floor. Zoe was there first, setting up the room so the three teams could have their own place to work.

I never found Dr Tenderfoot to ask him about the blank slips of paper. I'd have to remind myself to ask him the next time he showed up. I wasn't too worried though. The fire in my belly was driving me to win – not to understand why a man would fill his top hat with blank pieces of paper.

Carlyle was in one corner of the room with

the rest of his team – two kids dressed like pirates, singing shanties and swaying back and forth. It was as weird as it sounded.

It was also a much smaller team than I was expecting. The pirate threat was definitely on the way out.

Dante was in another corner of the room, all by himself. Zoe said he never bothered asking anyone to join his team.

My friends and I were all seated in our corner – Gidget, Slug, Brayden, Faith, Zoe and

Naomi. It was a huge team, but there wasn't a limit on how many members I could have. I figured the more we had, the better our chances were at building a robot that *actually* worked.

The room was divided up by three huge sheets hanging on lines like they were air-drying. Each team had their own corner of the science lab to work in. We could still hear everything going on in the room, but we couldn't see each other.

Naomi was in the middle of a conversation with Slug. 'Y'see? You'll do it every time.'

'Do what?' I asked, taking a seat.

Naomi looked at me with a blank expression. And then she made an ugly face.

I wasn't sure what was happening, so... I made an ugly face back at her.

Slug threw his arms up. 'Dude, you just proved her right!'

'What?' I said, confused.

'Ugly faces are contagious,' Naomi said smugly. 'I can make an ugly face at anyone in the school, and they'll throw one right back to

HERS IS KINDA CUTE. MINE IS JUST... WOW.

me. Sometimes I just sit in the cafeteria making ugly faces. Every single time, someone else makes one when they see me, whether they know it or not.'

'They're not contagious,' I said. 'I only did that because I knew what you were doing.'

'Riiiight,' Naomi said.

Gidget sat on one of the tall stools, staring at her phone. Without looking up, she said, 'So *she's* really on our team?'

'You mean me?' Naomi asked.

Gidget never took her eyes away from the phone. 'Bingo. No Scavengers allowed.'

'I'm not a Scavenger anymore,' Naomi said.

'What's a Scavenger?' Zoe asked.

'Nothing,' I said. Zoe still didn't know who the Scavengers were, and at that point, I didn't think it was important to tell her. The less she knew about them, the better off she was. 'Yes, Naomi's part of the team. She's smart, and she's cool, and she's gonna help out a ton.'

Gidget finally stopped thumb-jabbing her phone and glanced up. After a sigh, she said, 'Whatever.'

Naomi put her hands on her hips and cleared her throat. 'Can we move on? I've said sorry to Chase and you guys. Can we *please* just build a robot?'

Everyone nodded, but like they didn't have a choice.

Team Cooper was off to a good start.

That was sarcasm . . . just so you know.

If everyone was *this* unhappy about Naomi

74

being on the team, I dreaded telling them she was back in the ninja clan.

Zoe took the lead. 'Remember that we don't have to build a super awesome robot – just a robot that can do *something*, like blink or move.'

'Seems a little hard for sixth graders, doesn't it?' Slug asked.

'That's exactly the kind of thinking a losing team would have,' Gidget said. 'Don't even get it in your brain that we *can't* do it. All we need to focus on is *how* we'll do it.'

The fire in my belly grew stronger as I listened to my friends talk about how we weren't going to give up. It was one of the rare times we were able to work together as a group, and I knew that as long as we kept our heads up, almost nothing could stop us.

Except maybe the red and green ninjas.

Tuesday.
The Science lab
before School.

I got to school early the next morning. I used to struggle with waking up before school even *started*, but I was getting better at it. Plus, I wanted to get there before the rest of my team – y'know, lead by example and all that stuff. Tenderfoot Industries had provided parts for each team to use to build their robot. There were enough parts that none of the robots would be exactly the same.

After we studied the pieces, my team and I came up with our robot. It wasn't super complicated or anything, but we were proud of it – and I thought Dr Tenderfoot might even be a little impressed.

I spent most of the night drawing blueprints and sketches for the robot. With my background as a professional comic book reader, I thought I had come up with a sweet design.

The blueprints and sketches were rolled up into tubes that I stuck between my book bag and my back, making it look like I was carrying ninja swords.

The school was quiet when I walked into the lobby. Principal Davis was standing inside the entrance wearing his Tuesday suit. His hands were in his pockets, and he was staring at the parking lot outside.

When he noticed me, he snapped out of his trance. 'Cooper,' he said with a nod.

'Hey, Principal Davis,' I said.

'Better get upstairs,' he said. 'The rest of your team's already up there waiting for you.'

'They are?' I said, surprised. So much for being the first one there.

I shuffled past the principal and headed for the lift next to the cafeteria entrance.

The lift doors opened the instant I pushed the button. I stepped through the doors, and then pushed the button for the second floor.

'Oh, and Chase?' Principal Davis said from the lobby.

The doors to the lift hadn't shut yet. 'Hmm?' I said, lifting my chin.

'I'm impressed with your choice in teammates,' he said. 'It takes real maturity to forgive someone like that.'

Principal Davis must've been talking about Naomi. I wasn't sure how he knew what had gone down with me and Naomi.

'Thanks,' I said with a smile as the lift doors shut.

I pushed open the door to the science lab. Inside the room was a flurry of activity and excitement.

I couldn't see Carlyle's team because of the

sheets, but I could hear them *Yaaaar*-ing away as they banged metal against metal. If I didn't know it was them, I would've thought for sure that it was a buncha monkeys back there.

Dante's corner of the room was pretty quiet, but I could see the top of his head over the sheet. He was pacing back and forth, probably brainstorming.

And then there was my team, Team Cooper. Principal Davis was right – everyone was already there.

Zoe, Faith, Brayden, Gidget, Slug and Naomi sat in a circle talking about how we were going to build the robot for the competition.

Someone must've brought pancakes because everyone had a plate on their laps with a short stack of pancakes.

'Mmmm,' I said, taking the seat next to Naomi. 'Gimme some pancakes! Who brought 'em?'

'I did,' said a voice from behind me.

I recognised the voice immediately, and my stomach dropped.

It was Wyatt, and he was holding a plate of
pancakes meant for me. On top of his head was
a chef's hat. It was weird, but I *wasn't* surprised
that he was wearing it.

'Eat up,' Wyatt said.

I took the pancakes from him because I
didn't know what else to do. I smiled tightly as
I set the plate on my lap.

'Thaaaaaanks,' I whispered.

'No prob, Bob,' Wyatt said, wiping his hands

his apron. 'Oh! I almost forgot the whipped cream and syrup!'

And then Principal Davis's comment about forgiveness and my team made sense. He thought Wyatt was on my team.

Wyatt walked back to the counter. It looked like he'd hijacked that spot and turned it into his own kitchen. There were cartons of buttermilk, bowls of pancake batter, cracked eggshells, butter, whipped cream, syrup, and an electric griddle. Almost everything was covered in a thin layer of flour.

I leaned into the centre of my circle of friends. 'What the heck?' I whispered. 'Why's he here?'

Zoe covered her mouth with her hand and spoke through a mouthful of food. 'Dude, his pancakes are *amazing*. Like, seriously, they're cooked happiness!'

'For real,' Faith said.

Everyone else nodded.

'I mean, why's he even in here?' I asked, shoving a forkful of pancake into my mouth.

I gotta be honest. Wyatt had whipped up a

batch of killer pancakes. I tilted my head back and sank in my seat.

'See?' Zoe whispered. 'I *told* you they were awesome!'

'Fine,' I said. 'They're good, but you haven't answered my question yet!'

Zoe sat up straight to make sure Wyatt was still out of earshot. 'We let him hang out because of *pancakes*, but we also didn't make him leave because you're the team leader, so it's *your* job to get rid of him!'

I groaned and took another bite of pancake. I wasn't as polite as Zoe. I spoke with a mouthful of food. 'Whatever, I'll ask him to leave when he gets back with—'

'Ask who to leave?' Wyatt said, standing next to me with a can of whipped cream and a bottle of syrup.

'Ummmm,' I said, shovelling another bite of pancake into my mouth. Wyatt's body slumped as he lowered the whipped cream and syrup.

'You're talking about me, aren't you?' he said quietly. 'You wanna ask me to leave?'

The group stared at me, waiting for my answer.

But before I could say anything, Wyatt spoke. 'C'mon, dude, *please* let me be on your team. I'll do anything to help. Whatever you need! I'll be the coffee guy! Or the pancake guy! I know we've butted heads before, but I'm tellin' ya that I *want* to change! It's just that...I don't... I don't really have any friends anymore.'

No one else knew Wyatt had lost his ninja clan. I knew better than my friends what Wyatt was feeling, and I couldn't help but feel sorry for him.

Wyatt grew impatient and pointed at Naomi. 'I mean, c'mon! You let *her* on the team! She tried to ruin your life! All I did was...well, never mind what *I* did. If Naomi's on the team, why can't I be?'

Naomi looked away, her cheeks red.

'Bro!' Wyatt said. 'You gotta be like water!'

I looked Wyatt dead in the eye. 'What'd you say?'

'Be like water,' he repeated.

A chill ran down my spine. Real Wyatt had said the same thing as Dream Wyatt.

But... Wyatt *wasn't* wrong. I couldn't shun him after welcoming Naomi back with open arms, could I?

Shutting my eyes, I took the last bite of my pancakes. 'Fine,' I whispered.

'I'm sorry,' Gidget said, leaning closer to me. 'What was that?'

'Open your earballs, ya old lady,' Wyatt said to Gidget.

Gidget rested her phone on her lap and spoke calmly while she looked at Wyatt. 'I have a soul-crushing comeback for that, but I'm gonna stop myself from saying it 'cause it'll wreck you so bad that your *children* will feel the burn. They'll *cry* themselves to sleep, and when you see their tears... you'll remember *me*.'

'Jeez...' Wyatt whispered.

'She's tellin' the truth, man,' Slug warned Wyatt.

My eyes were still shut. 'Wyatt's on the team.'

The rest of the team started talking at the same time, shocked and unhappy at my decision.

'Guys, it's fine,' Wyatt said sadly. 'I get it. I know when I'm not wanted. I'll just... get some breakfast or something... by myself.'

As he shuffled towards the science lab door, I could tell how hurt he was.

And the war that was going on in my head was driving me crazy!

Wyatt had been the bad guy since the first day of school. He'd been against me at every twist and turn! He'd done *so many* bad things and I should've been happy about him walking away, but I wasn't...

Everyone deserved second chances, didn't they? And *third* and *fourth* chances, I guess?

What if that was the point in Wyatt's life that defined if he was a good guy or a bad guy? If I let him leave, he'd be hurt and probably carry even more of a grudge against me... but if I let him on the team, then maybe, *just maybe*, he'd stop being such a jerk.

My friends returned their attention to the project for the competition. Wyatt was at the door.

I sighed heavily because I knew what I had to do. 'Wait!' I said.

Wyatt glanced over his shoulder. The way he did it was creepy, and not helpful in making him seem like less of a villain, but I ignored it since that's kinda his whole thing.

'You can be on the team,' I said. 'But you can't sit around. You gotta help us build this robot, alright?'

Wyatt turned, standing up straight. He marched back to our circle a little *too* victoriously.

'Thanks, bro,' he said, his voice bright and loud. He pulled up a seat up, flipped it backwards, and sat on it, resting his arms on the back of the chair. 'So … when do we start?'

As if in answer, the door to the science lab opened. One of the kitchen staff peeked her head in and pointed at Wyatt.

'You!' she said accusingly. 'You left the

kitchen before you paid for those ingredients! I said you could take what you wanted as long as you *bought* them!'

Wyatt leaned back, stretching his arms like he had just woken up. 'Oh,' he said with a smirk. 'Chase'll be paying. The pancakes were for my... I mean, *his* team.'

The woman looked at me, waiting for an answer.

I sighed. 'Sure,' I said, digging my wallet out of my book bag. 'I got it.'

Wyatt wasn't exactly *lying*.

The pancakes *were* for the team...

... right?

Tuesday.
Lunch.

My friends weren't happy with my decision to let Wyatt on the team, but they didn't fuss anymore about it.

It helped that I vouched for Wyatt too. I told them that it was my own mistake to make, but I felt like he really wanted to start a new chapter in his life. I hoped I wasn't wrong.

Zoe even came up to me afterwards and apologised, telling me that giving Wyatt a shot on the team was the 'grown-up' thing to do. Then she slugged me in the arm, like, *way* too hard, like she always does.

Faith would probably slug my arm in the same spot later in the day. Those two seemed to always punch me in the same spot on the same day, and repeatedly... like they had planned it...

Aaaand I'm just realising now that they probably *do* plan it. I'm such a noob sometimes.

Once I got my food from the kitchen, I stepped into the cafeteria to find a seat. I was still stuffed from the pancakes that Wyatt made before school, so I opted for the student favourite – French fries with mayonnaise and tomato sauce, along with a bowl of broccoli cheese soup. Blanketing the soup with pepper was optional, but I always did it.

Team Cooper was sitting at a table across the room, waving at me to join them, so I started walking in their direction.

About halfway across the cafeteria, I heard Wyatt call out my name. He was sitting on the stage with his legs crossed. His girlfriend, Olivia Jones, was sitting next to him, taking a bite from a cheese-deprived cheeseburger.

I nodded at him, but continued towards my friends.

'Wait,' Wyatt said. 'I have some things to talk to you about.'

Stopping in place, I looked back to where my friends were seated. There was still plenty of time left for lunch, so I guess I had a few minutes to stop and hear what Wyatt had to say.

Resting my tray on the stage, I hopped up, and slid closer to Wyatt and Olivia. It was a completely new feeling for me to *choose* to sit near Wyatt.

I had to get outta my bubble, right?

Olivia smiled her awkward smile. She had got braces since the last time I talked to her. 'Hi, Chase.'

I smiled back. If you've followed my life at all, you'll know how weird it was that Wyatt and Olivia were being nice to me, or even talking to me at all.

'This isn't easy for me,' Wyatt said. Olivia put her hand on his as if to comfort him. 'But

THIS IS
OLIVIA
THIS IS WHAT
HAPPENS WHEN
SHE FAKES A
SMILE...

I wanted to thank you for letting me join your team.'

'Yeah,' Olivia said. 'It's pretty cool of you.'

'Well, I'm a pretty cool guy,' I joked.

'Did you hear that the mystery prize is a million dollars?' Olivia said.

'No way!' I said. 'A million-dollar prize for a sixth-grade robot project?'

'Tenderfoot's a billionaire,' Wyatt said.

'A million bucks is nothing to him. I'm buyin' a boat when I win – I mean, when *we* win.'

I had my doubts about the rumour, but it *was* pretty exciting.

I took a chance and asked a hard question. 'What was up with those ninjas yesterday? Why'd they corner you and throw us into the library?'

Wyatt's face tensed, but he quickly relaxed. 'I'm only talking to you about it because you let me on your team,' he said. 'You remember how the red and green ninja clans were trying to steal our masks, right?'

Olivia looked sad.

'Right,' I said. 'Whoever got our masks would be the leaders of those ninja clans.'

'The green ninjas have their new leader because they got your mask last week,' Wyatt said. 'The red ninjas have their leader already, but they still want to send a message by taking my mask.'

'What's the message?' I asked.

'Get lost,' Olivia said, answering for Wyatt.

'Do you know who the leaders are?' I said.

'No clue.' Wyatt shook his head. 'I showed up to training one day and was booted right out of my own ninja clan.'

'Did you do something that made them mad?' I said.

Wyatt took a deep breath. 'My red ninja clan had got too big for me to control by myself. The rest of my ninjas knew it, too. They questioned my leadership skills and wanted to do things I didn't want to do.'

'Like what?' I said, dipping some fries in my broccoli cheese soup, and then shoving them into my mouth. Hey, don't knock it till ya try it.

'Dumb things,' Olivia said. 'Like they wanted to start a website and sell t-shirts and junk!'

'We're a ninja clan!' Wyatt said. 'Not a business!'

I continued chewing on my awesome broccoli cheese fries, nodding as Wyatt went on.

'So I guess everyone thought they could do a better job of being a leader,' Wyatt said. 'And

that's exactly what happened – one day,
everyone stopped listening to me and started
doing whatever they wanted. There wasn't
anyone loyal to me after that. Nobody sided
with me. And that's when I lost control
completely.'

'But what about the kid who ordered
everyone to steal our masks?' I said.

'Nobody was listening to *me*,' Wyatt said, 'but
when *someone else* stood up and spoke, they

were all ears. The group was falling apart because it had nobody to lead it, and they knew it. They just needed a little direction from someone who *wasn't* me.'

'And that's when they gave the order to take our masks,' I added.

'Not quite,' Wyatt said. 'I *thought* that stealing my mask would choose the new leader for the red ninjas, but I was wrong. They already had their leader. They just wanted to boot me from the game.'

'And then someone decided that stealing *your* mask would be just as awesome,' Olivia added, 'which is when the green ninja clan was born.'

I shrugged my shoulders. 'No big deal. I got a million ninja masks in my locker.'

'The red and green ninja clans are basically sister clans,' Wyatt said. 'They're working together, but wearing different colours.'

'Holiday ninjas,' I whispered, shovelling more fries into my mouth.

Olivia snickered.

Wyatt took another deep breath, and said,

'Which brings us to the reason why I wanted to be on your robot team.'

'Of course,' I said hesitantly, worried that I might've fallen for another one of Wyatt's tricks.

'No!' he said defensively. 'It's not like that. I honestly want to get on your good side, because...well, I need your help.'

'Go on...'

'I want to work *with* you to figure out what to do about the red and green ninjas,' he said. 'Letting them continue is just crazysauce, right? I mean, those kids are *dangerous*!'

'So what do you wanna do?' I asked, not sure if I wanted to hear the answer.

Wyatt smiled, and it was genuine. 'I just want things to go back to normal, like the good ol' days, with only the red ninjas versus the black ninjas.'

'Normal?' I said, laughing. 'Normal for you is only *one* enemy? Normal for me is *no* enemies!'

'I'm not saying we should be enemies!' Wyatt said. 'I'm saying that maybe we should team up and be...*frenemies*. C'mon, think about it. You wanna deal with *two* ninja clans who are out to get you?'

I hated that Wyatt was *kind of* making sense. I had no idea who the leaders of the new ninja clans were, but at least I *knew* Wyatt.

Wyatt's plan was to make it so it was only his ninja clan against mine, but I needed more than that if I was gonna help him.

Finally, I said, 'I'll help you under one condition.'

'Name it,' Wyatt said seriously.

'Once we figure this thing out with those other two ninja clans, we stop being enemies,' I said. 'We don't have to be friends, but we're definitely not enemies.'

'You're telling me to give up my ninja clan?' Wyatt asked, narrowing his eyes.

'No,' I said. 'Two ninja clans can exist in the school without ever bumping into each other. You leave mine alone. That's all I want.'

Wyatt didn't hesitate. 'Deal,' he said.

Olivia swooned over her boyfriend. 'I'm so proud of you, babe!'

Wyatt leaned back, smiling smugly.

And for the first time in a long time, I saw a glimmer of hope for the future. A truce with Wyatt would be an epic win for me. Of course, there was always the chance it would turn into an epic fail – Wyatt can be shady like that.

All I could do was hope for the best.

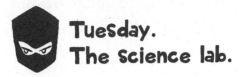 **Tuesday.**
The science lab.

Naomi met me in the lobby, next to the statue of James Buchanan, and together we headed to the science lab.

'Yo,' Naomi said.

'Whassup?' I replied.

'Nothing. I just wanted to walk into the science lab *with* you.'

I paused. 'Because you feel like everyone hates you?'

Naomi didn't answer, which meant I was right.

'They don't,' I said. 'They might not be

happy with you right now, but they'd never *hate* you.'

'They might. Kids can change their minds about people.'

'You just gotta give it a little time. It'll be weird at first, but once they see that you're the real deal, they'll warm back up to you,' I said.

Naomi smiled. 'You really think it's that easy?'

I nodded, smiling.

'I don't even know why I'm so stressed about this,' Naomi said, laughing nervously. 'I thought I didn't care about what others think about me.'

I laughed. 'I'm pretty sure I'll always care about what people think of me. I can try to ignore it, but that doesn't mean I don't care.'

'At least with Wyatt on the team,' Naomi said, 'everyone has something *else* to focus on besides me. It's cool that you let him on Team Cooper. I couldn't do it. I'd be too paranoid about him.'

'Well, I'm not gonna lie,' I said. 'I've got a terrible feeling in my butt about it.'

'What? Your butt?' Naomi asked, frowning.

'Yeah,' I said. 'Y'know, a butt feeling.'

Naomi laughed so hard she choked a little. '*Gut* feeling! You got a terrible *gut* feeling about it!'

'Ohhhh,' I said, embarrassed by a *lifetime* of saying it wrong. 'I'm an idiot.'

Naomi tried to hide her smile, but she couldn't.

A minute later, we were standing outside the science lab. Pushing open the door, I let Naomi go in first.

From the moment I entered the room, all I could hear were the sounds of hammers and drills.

My team was to the right, hunched over the blueprints. Wyatt was in the middle of the group.

Even though I couldn't see the other teams, I knew that Carlyle's team only had a few kids on it. I heard the voices of two or three students from his side of the room.

Dante's area was super quiet. Like, dead quiet.

If I hadn't seen his shadow moving behind the sheet, I would've sworn there was nobody there.

'Is Dante still on his own?' I asked Naomi.

She nodded. 'I think so. Zoe said something about Dante being the quiet type. Not creepy loner, but just…quiet.'

'She said the same thing to me too,' I said. 'That Dante never even tried to get anyone else on his team.'

'Oh, I heard he asked some peeps, but they said no,' Naomi said.

I sighed. 'Bummer.'

Naomi and I grabbed a couple of empty chairs and joined the rest of our team.

Zoe chewed on the end of a pencil as she held my blueprints in front of her. Faith was next to her pointing at different spots of my drawings and quietly commenting on them.

Gidget was busy tapping away on her phone, researching for the project. Slug was slouched over with his hands on his round belly. He looked like he had just finished off his tenth plate at a pizza buffet.

Brayden was next to him, munching away on some kind of tortilla filled with cheese and meat. It was too thin to be a taco, which meant it was probably...

'Quesadillas,' Slug slurred with his eyes half open, pronouncing it *kay-suh-dill-ahs*. 'Wyatt made chicken quesadillas. I might've had one too many...'

'How many did you eat?' I asked.

'Eight,' Slug answered, breathing heavily.

'Eight triangles?' I said.

Slug shook his head. 'No...eight *full* quesadillas.'

'Dude,' I said, my jaw dropping to the floor. 'That's, like, um...four times eight... *thirty-four pieces*!'

Naomi quickly corrected me. 'Thirty-two.'

'Thirty-*two*!' I repeated.

'This kid can pack 'em away!' Wyatt said, bringing another plate of quesadillas to the group.

'Gidgy...' Slug said, reaching for his twin sister, who was scooting away from his greasy

fingers. 'I might need a stomach transplant after this.'

'Gross,' she said. 'Don't touch me.'

'Gidgyyyyyy!' Slug groaned. 'We're *twins*! Your stomach is an exact match for mine! Only *you* can save me! I only need *half* of it. It'll grow back!'

'Dude,' Gidget said, raising an eyebrow. 'You can't have my stomach.'

'But what if I *need* it?' Slug whined, sliding lower in his chair. 'You're just gonna—'

And then Slug let out the grossest burp I'd ever heard in my life. It was loud, and it was bad. Like, my eyes started watering.

Slug instantly sat up in his seat with a smile beaming across his face. 'All better,' he said, reaching for another quesadilla. 'Mmmm, gimme, gimme, gimme!'

Gidget shook her head at Slug, looking disgusted. 'Hashtag *so* gross.'

Slug stuffed the loaded tortilla into his mouth and chomped loudly, leaning closer to his sister to annoy her. 'Did you hear my face fart?'

'Get out!' Gidget said laughing loudly as she pushed her elbow into Slug to keep him away.

'Wyatt makes the best quesadillas,' Faith said. 'We've appointed him the official chef for Team Cooper.'

Wyatt nodded and faked the kind of laugh a politician would have. 'Hey, I'll take what I can get,' he said, presenting a quesadilla to Faith.

'I thank ye, kind sir,' Faith said as she took a tortilla off the plate.

'My pleasure, m'lady,' Wyatt replied, nodding.

Even Zoe chuckled, shaking her head at Wyatt as she took a quesadilla from him.

I thought it was gross.

It was shocking how quickly my team had warmed up to Wyatt. Not that I cared ... I just thought it was gonna take a little more time.

And then I noticed Olivia sitting way off to the side. She was on a seat that was backed against the wall. And she did *not* look happy.

'Why's Olivia over there?' I asked. 'And why's she glaring at us?'

Brayden sat up, pushing his chest out, and beating on it twice like a caveman. 'She's allergic to my cologne,' he said proudly. 'She has a sneezing fit whenever she gets close.'

'Ironic, isn't it?' Zoe said. 'The thing you're spraying yourself to *attract* girls is actually *repelling* them.'

'I know, right?' Brayden said, rolling his eyes. 'But I've allowed myself time to learn how to use the cologne properly.'

'Allowed yourself time?' Zoe repeated,

lowering the blueprints to get a better look at Brayden. 'Until what? Until you woo all the ladies in the world with your musk?'

Brayden snapped two fingers and pointed at Zoe. 'Totes,' he said slyly.

Zoe did her best to hide her smile. 'Oh, jeez.'

I looked at Olivia again.

'I don't mind,' I said, 'but why is she here? If Brayden's cologne is makin' her sneeze, why would she stick around?'

OLIVIA'S POUTY FACE ☺!!!

'She's here for me,' Wyatt said, waving at Olivia. She didn't wave back. 'Her presence comforts me.'

'That's such a weird way to say that,' I said. But I looked at Faith and she smiled at me, and I knew exactly what Wyatt meant.

'I vouch for her,' Wyatt said. 'Just like you vouched for me. How's that?'

'Okay,' I said, not really bothered either way. 'She can stay. As long as she doesn't mess up our flow.'

Wyatt nodded seriously. 'Of course,' he said. 'She's cool.'

The door to the science lab swung open, and someone in a Tenderfoot Industries shirt wheeled in a flat-screen television.

'Students,' the employee said. 'Students, if you could please look up here, Dr Tenderfoot has recorded a message for you.'

Everyone in the room stopped what they were doing and stepped out from behind their sheets. Carlyle was with his pirate buddies. Dante was on his own, covered in grease.

The employee took a small cassette tape from his shirt pocket and inserted it into a slot on the television.

The screen flipped on and showed Dr Ashley Tenderfoot's face, complete with old-fashioned moustache, top hat, and a monocle over his right eye.

'Hello,' Tenderfoot said. 'First of all, I'd like to congratulate *all* of you for being selected for the competition. I'm sure that Carlyle, Dante

and Chase have chosen their teams wisely, so be proud if you're listening to this message.'

Some kids looked at Dante because he didn't have a team standing behind him. He was obviously embarrassed.

With all the excitement of the last twenty-four hours, I had completely forgotten about Tenderfoot selecting the team leaders from his top hat. The slips of paper in his hat were blank, and if you asked me, that rated pretty highly on the mystery scale.

My brain was so busy running that I missed the rest of Tenderfoot's video message. All I caught was the very last part.

'…and I thank you again for playing your part in this historic competition,' he said. Tenderfoot tipped his top hat down, and the video stopped.

The employee from Tenderfoot Industries removed the cassette and pushed it into his front pocket. Wheeling the television out the door, he looked over his shoulder, said 'Good day,' and left the room.

The other teams moved back behind their bed sheets and continued their work.

Faith said what everyone else was thinking. 'Tenderfoot's weird.'

'Who records a message like that?' Wyatt said.

'Dr Tenderfoot is a super busy man,' Zoe said defensively. 'I'm just happy that he sent us *any* kind of message.'

I pondered for a moment... That's such an adult-sounding thing to say, isn't it? Pretend I have an old-school gentleman's voice. 'Mmmmm, yes, I *pondered* for a moment...'

The tape had me thinking. I turned to Zoe. 'Remember when I was talking about hiding messages to our future relatives in the school? Like, a hundred years from now, I could talk to my great-grandkids or whatever?'

Zoe sighed, shutting her eyes. 'Yeaaaaaaaaah,' she said.

'I could record videos like Tenderfoot did!' I said, excited. 'I could hide them all over the school and send my great-grandchildren on treasure hunts and stuff!'

Slug nodded, scratching his chin. 'I like the way you think, mister.'

'No way,' Wyatt said abruptly. 'In a hundred years, cassette tapes won't even exist. I'm surprised Tenderfoot even used one! Think about it – do you send messages using morse code?'

Gidget was the one who answered, still jabbing at her phone with her thumbs. 'Um, no way, dude.'

'Exactly,' Wyatt said. 'Let's say you *did* leave a bunch of tapes hidden in the school, and your great-great-great-grandkids found them.'

'Okay?' I said.

'They wouldn't even know what to do with them!' Wyatt said, and then he pretended to inspect an invisible cassette in his hand. 'They'd be like, "What the heck is this thing?"'

'I'm sure cassette tapes will still be used,' Brayden said.

'Do you know what the very first records looked like?' Wyatt asked.

Slug perked up. 'What's a record?'

Wyatt pointed at Slug. 'Exactly,' he said.

'One, most kids don't even know what a record is, and two, the very first records looked like tubes. Not the flat discs people are familiar with.'

'But people can still play records,' Naomi said.

'Give it another fifty years,' Wyatt said. 'Records won't even exist anymore, except maybe to hardcore antique collectors.'

Slug raised his hand. 'Wait, I'm still not entirely sure what a *record* is. You can play it? Like, in a game or something?'

Gidget lowered her head, rubbing the bridge of her nose. 'Dude ...'

'In a hundred years, I bet there will be something *way* cooler than cassettes,' Wyatt said. 'They'll probably be beaming information right into their eyeballs.'

I nodded. Having information beamed right into my eyeballs *did* sound pretty awesome ... maybe Tenderfoot Industries was already working on that.

Oh man, how *cool* would that be?

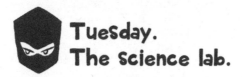

Tuesday.
The science lab.

After our cassette-tape conversation, my team split into four groups. Zoe and Faith dealt with the moving parts of our robot. Slug and Brayden worked on the shell of the robot because, c'mon, the robot had to look *awesome*. Gidget and Naomi were figuring out what parts we still needed.

And finally, Wyatt and I were in charge of refining the mechanics of the robot – like trying to make it work better with fewer parts and stuff.

Dante's voice exploded from behind his sheet. 'Stupid machine! Just *work* already! I'm doing everything right, why won't you just work?'

'Whoa,' Slug said. 'Someone's having problems.'

Dante's shadow moved back and forth. And then he raised his foot and kicked at another large shadow, knocking it over. The sound of screws and metal parts hitting the floor filled the air.

'Way to go, Dante,' he said to himself. 'Messed things up again, didn't you? It's not the robot's fault it doesn't work, it's *yours*.'

We all watched as Dante's shadow stood perfectly still. After a moment, he walked out from behind the sheet and left the room.

'Yikes,' Brayden said.

Wyatt slid a chair next to mine and flipped it around again, sitting on it backwards with his arms on the backrest. Quietly, he asked, 'So what do you think we should do about the red and green ninja clans?'

'Hmm?' I hummed. 'Oh, I don't know. I haven't thought about it yet.'

'Time's runnin' out, Chase,' Wyatt said. 'The longer it takes us to make a move, the larger those two ninja clans get.'

'Make a move?' I said. 'What kind of move are you talking about?'

'I've got a few ideas.'

I glanced over my shoulder. The rest of my team was behind me, working on their section of the robot, and there I was, talking ninja stuff with my ... *frenemy*.

'What're your ideas?' I asked.

'Well,' Wyatt said, sitting up straight. 'I have

three ideas. The first one is that we find the leaders of the two ninja clans and beat the *snot* out of them.'

'Nope,' I said quickly. 'Not an option. Next.'

Wyatt clenched his jaw, but continued. 'You and I go undercover. We'll sneak into the red and green ninja clans and take them over from the inside.'

'Because it's *that* easy,' I said sarcastically.

'Fine,' Wyatt said. 'My last idea – we figure out who the leaders of the clans are and set a trap for them. When we catch 'em, we'll steal *their* masks and humiliate 'em by covering them in syrup and feathers!'

'Where would we get the feathers?' I asked, genuinely curious.

'From pillows, dummy!' Wyatt said, lightly slapping my arm with the back of his hand.

'While that *does* sound amazing,' I said, 'I'm pretty sure it's a terrible idea. But I'm going to steal that syrup-and-feather prank for myself and get Brayden or Slug with it someday.'

Wyatt slouched forward. 'Alright then, what do *you* think we should do?'

'I don't know,' I answered honestly. 'Maybe…we should find them and *talk* to them about what's happening.'

'Oh, yeah?' Wyatt said. 'And what're you gonna say? Please stop messing with us?'

I paused. 'Yeah.'

'But what if their plan *isn't* to mess with us?' Wyatt said. 'What if they're up to something else? Something bigger and badder?'

It was possible. Most of the stuff I'd been caught up in this year had nothing to do with *me*. There was always a different goal. The hairs on my arms stood on end.

'Where do they train?' I said, watching the rest of my team.

'No clue,' Wyatt said. 'We used to be in the

overgrown greenhouse, but when I checked this morning, it was empty.'

'So the first thing we have to do is figure out where they're hiding,' I said.

Wyatt tapped his fingers on the back of the chair and swayed like he was dancing to music I couldn't hear. He was excited.

'They could be anywhere in the school,' I said. 'This building is like a flippin' maze with all kinds of hidden hallways and tunnels. But the question is *how* do we find them?'

'Let's make *them* find *us*,' Wyatt suggested.

'I like that,' I said. 'Okay, how?'

'Bait,' Wyatt said.

'Okaaaay…' I said, suddenly uneasy.

'We'll use *you* as bait,' he said with a smirk.

'Ugh,' I groaned as Wyatt stepped away to work out the plans with Olivia. 'What have I got myself into?'

 **Wednesday.
The lobby.**

It was early. And cold. And again, I was at
school *before* it started.

In the lobby, I stopped to blow hot air into
my hands.

Principal Davis and my homeroom teacher,
Mrs Robinson, were walking out of the front
office. When they saw me, they smiled and
waved. Mrs Robinson was carrying a bunch of
black balloons, which were floating above her
head.

'Greetings,' a girl's voice said from the corner
of the lobby.

Spinning on my heel, I saw Olivia on a bench.

Normal kids don't say, 'Greetings,' but Olivia wasn't exactly normal.

Popping to her feet, Olivia said, 'Wyatt seeks your presence.'

See what I mean?

'Uh, yeah, I know,' I said. 'We were supposed to meet. Where is he?'

'I'll take you to him,' she said as she started down the hall.

Uneasy. That's how I felt about the whole thing. Wyatt found his way onto my team. And now he was *seeking* my presence. It was like he was giving me orders.

Olivia stopped at a door next to the lift. I'd never see the door before in my life even though I walked by it a million times a day.

Pulling the door open, Olivia nodded towards it, gesturing me to go in first.

I looked around to see if anyone else was in the hallway – not to make sure we were alone, but to make sure someone was a witness to the last place Chase Cooper had been seen.

There was nobody.

'You go first,' I said.

'No,' Olivia said. 'It's polite to allow you to go first. I only wish to be in your favour.'

'Stop talking like that!' I said.

Olivia said nothing as she waited for me to go first.

Holding my breath, I stepped into the mysterious room. Once inside, I found out that it wasn't a room, but a long corridor. The walls were grey brick and the floor was smooth concrete, which made it look like an unfinished basement.

'What is this?' I asked Olivia.

She stepped past me. 'The veins of Buchanan. These hallways give people access to any part of the school. It's in case of an emergency. Kids will be able to get out faster through here.'

'Secret hallways,' I said. 'This school's got everything.'

Olivia looked over her shoulder. 'You haven't even scratched the surface yet.'

'You mean there's more?' I asked, following Olivia as she turned at one of the corners.

'Oh, yeah,' she said, running her fingers along the grey bricks. 'You think you know the secrets of this school? Hardly.'

I wasn't sure whether to be excited or scared at that thought.

Olivia stopped at the end of the hallway, where it opened up to a large room.

At the centre of the room was a short brick wall that formed a circle on the floor. At one point in time it must've been used as a well. The top of the well was boarded up though, so there wasn't any danger of Timmy falling down it.

Get it? Timmy? Lassie? No? Okay, moving on ...

Wyatt was sitting on the side of the well. 'Chase, old friend! I'm glad you could make it.'

I shuddered when he called me 'old friend'.

'What d'you mean you're glad I could make it?' I said. 'We *agreed* to meet.'

'I know, I know,' Wyatt said, patting at the air with both hands. 'I'm just sayin' that I'm glad you're here.'

SOME CRAZY SECRET ROOM WITH A WELL.

I leaned against the cold brick wall near the entrance. 'I'm here,' I said. 'What's the plan?'

'The plan is to use you as bait,' Wyatt said.

'I already know that,' I said. 'But *how*?'

Wyatt sighed with a worried look on his face. His forehead wrinkled. 'Good question... I guess we could put you on a pedestal in the lobby. Maybe make a game of it? Throw a bunch of baseballs at a target. If you hit the target, Chase falls into a pool of water?'

'Seriously?' I said.

'You're right,' Wyatt said. 'Too complicated.'

'Ya think?' Olivia said from the entrance.

'Babe,' Wyatt said. 'You know my love language is words, and when you make sarcastic comments like that, it hurts my feelings.'

Olivia's eyes softened. 'Sorry, baby. Smooches!' she said, blowing a kiss to Wyatt.

Wyatt bobbed back and forth, and then he caught the invisible kiss. He smiled as he put it in his front pocket.

Oh my god. Watching Wyatt and Olivia have a moment ... If it was possible for a brain to barf, mine was about ten seconds away from doing it. It was going to shoot out of my *ears*.

Olivia smiled. 'Good luck,' she said as she left Wyatt and me alone.

'Is she gonna help?' I asked.

Wyatt shook his head. 'No, she has something else to do.'

'What?' I said.

'Talk to a teacher about homework or something? I dunno,' Wyatt said.

I pushed myself off the wall. 'Let's think simple, okay? We don't know where they're training, but we know they've got eyes all over the school.'

'Probably,' Wyatt said. He snapped his fingers as an idea popped into his head. 'How about you run around the hallways wearing your ninja mask? Those kids are probably always looking for *you*, right?'

For a second, I wanted to argue that it was an idiotic idea, but it actually wasn't. I couldn't think of a better, simpler way to get the red or green ninja clan to come after me.

Finally, I nodded. 'Fine.'

'Good,' Wyatt said, standing. 'Let's go catch some ninjas!'

Wednesday.
The Dungeon.

I was on my own in the lower level of the school, better known as the Dungeon – cold, wet, gross.

I'm gonna be honest with you ... I wasn't *not* scared.

Being alone in the dungeon was as scary as running through the woods at two in the morning. The creepy buzzing lights didn't help either. Some of them were even burned out, which meant sometimes walking in almost complete darkness.

'Stupid, stupid, stupid,' I sang to myself, trying to keep a jolly melody.

A locker slammed. I spun around, sure that I was going to see a monster come at me, but I was alone.

I took my ninja mask from my hood and slipped it over my face.

Step by step, I made my way deeper into the dungeon. Once I turned the corner, the light from the stairwell was gone, and I was at the point of no return.

Most of the hallway lights in front of me were busted, leaving the hallway drenched in black shadows.

I was beginning to regret *everything*.

Something behind me hit the floor, barely making a sound, like someone had softly dropped a towel or something.

I froze, leaning against the lockers. I turned to see what was behind me, doing my best to stay calm.

Nothing was there.

The noise came again ... and again ... and again and again, getting closer, but there wasn't anything in the hallway.

My legs forgot how to be legs. They were doing their best impression of tree trunks! My teeth were grinding as the sounds came closer. I was in a nightmare!

My voice stopped in my throat as I stared at the empty hallway. Finally, I managed to squeeze out, 'C'mon!'

And then, like a video game, my legs unpaused and I was sprinting away as fast as my thin legs could take me.

The muffled sounds behind me kept up. It only made sense that Wyatt's plan worked, and that the monster in the dark was actually a ninja.

With every hallway I turned down, I ran faster. The few footsteps chasing me turned into *many* footsteps. Player three had entered the game.

Ahead was a door that was left wide open. It was the only door in the Dungeon that hadn't been locked, so I did what any sixth grade ninja would do... I dove in headfirst.

Luckily for me, the room was empty. Unluckily for me, there was only *one* way out of it, and that was back through the door I had just entered.

Sliding under the teacher's desk, I tucked myself away, hoping the ninjas would walk past me. If they did, then I'd have a chance at escaping back through the door.

And if they didn't? Well, I could see the headlines now... *Sixth Grader Chase Cooper Disappears. Nobody Cares.*

At the front of the room, I saw the shadows of two ninjas. They always travelled in packs of two or three.

I sat completely still under the teacher's desk. My heart was pounding so hard it felt like it was trying to escape from my chest.

There was a red ninja and a green one. They were working together.

So much for the plan. I was supposed to lure the ninjas out of hiding so Wyatt and I could figure out where they were training. Instead, I was cowering under a desk, hoping that the bell would ring.

'Where'd he go?' the first ninja said. It was a boy.

'I don't know. Is there another way out?' the other ninja said. A girl.

'Not that I see.'

'Lemme turn the light on.'

'No! We work in the dark. *Always* in the dark.'

'*Actually* that's really bad for your eyes,' the girl said with attitude.

'There you go again! This is why everyone calls you "Actually"! You're always correcting people.'

'Wait...' the girl said. 'What's that?'

'What's what?'

'*That*... under the teacher's desk,' she answered.

Oh no...

Their footsteps got closer and closer.

I had no choice. I rolled out from the desk and ran straight for the front door, but in my confusion, I had run to the *back* of the room.

'There!' the girl shouted. 'He's cornered himself!'

'Noob!' the other ninja shouted.

I slammed into the back wall. My arm got caught up in long strings, which wrapped themselves around my hand. I didn't know what was going on, but it couldn't have been good.

The red and green ninjas slid to a stop.

I stared at their shadows, trying to untangle myself.

'He's not alone,' the boy said.

The girl ninja took a step backwards. 'Well played, Chase... You think you can trick the two of us, but we're *smarter* than that. We know when we're outnumbered.'

Outnumbered? The two ninjas ran back to the door, sliding across desks, and doing cartwheels to show off.

At the door, the girl ninja turned around. From the lights in the hallway, I saw that her ninja outfit was green. 'We'll meet again, Chase. And when we do, we'll bring more of *our* friends.'

The green ninja raised a small ball, and then she slammed it into the floor. A cloud of chalk dust burst at her feet. When the fog lifted, she was gone.

I leaned my head back, bumping it against the wall. I was alone again.

The strings around my arm tugged at something above my head.

'Hello?' Wyatt said from the doorway like he had teleported there.

'Dude,' I said. 'Did you see the other ninjas out there?'

Wyatt leaned back and scanned the halls. 'Nope. No one else out here.'

Was it a coincidence that Wyatt appeared so quickly after the other ninjas disappeared? Or was I just being paranoid?

'Wait.' He paused. 'I thought we said you were gonna come down here alone.'

'I *am* alone,' I said, still against the back wall.

'No, you're not,' Wyatt said, stepping through the door. 'There's, like, five ninjas behind you!'

'What're talking about?' I asked, annoyed. 'There's nobody else in here except you and me!'

'And the ninjas behind you,' Wyatt said,
flipping on the light.

I squeezed my eyes shut because the lights
hurt them.

'Oh, my bad,' Wyatt said. 'You *are* alone.'

Forcing my eyelids open,
I looked at the strings
that were wrapped
around my arm.
They led to five
black balloons
that floated right
next to my head.

On the whiteboard
at the front of the
room was a message
that read, 'Happy 40th Birthday, Mr Lopez!'
A cake covered in black frosting sat on top of
his desk.

I freed myself from the clutches of the
balloons and took my mask off. 'I got cornered.
Those ninjas must've thought these black
balloons were my other ninjas.'

Wyatt snorted. 'I thought they were too.'

'I got super lucky then,' I said.

'But hey!' Wyatt said, grinning. 'Our plan worked! You got their attention!'

My blood boiled. 'It didn't work at all, dude! I got them to chase me, but we still don't know where they're hiding!'

'Fine,' Wyatt said. 'Maybe it didn't turn out the way we…'

I looked at Wyatt. 'The way we what?'

Wyatt didn't answer. He was staring at a spot on the floor next to the door. Kneeling down, Wyatt slid his hand across the linoleum.

'Look at all these tiny pebbles,' he said.

The pebbles were small and speckled black and grey.

'This might not have been pointless after all,' Wyatt said. 'Looks like we just found a solid clue.'

'You're just gonna take that back to the lab,' I said sarcastically. 'Study it under a microscope, and then cross reference the evidence to figure out which quarry it came from?'

'If you'd rather be bait again...' Wyatt trailed off, smirking.

'No, no!' I said. 'Clues are good! I'm all *about* clues, dude!'

If studying clues meant I didn't have to get hunted by a bunch of ninjas, then I was gonna study clues like it was my job.

 **Wednesday.
Lunch.**

I spent the rest of the morning looking over my shoulder every couple of seconds. It sounds paranoid, but when you're worrying about ninjas sneak-attacking you, checking every couple of seconds might not even be enough.

I scanned the cafeteria for my friends. I didn't have much of an appetite so all I got was a juice and a chocolate-chip biscuit.

'Outta the way, mouthbreather!' Gidget joked from behind me.

I stepped aside to let Gidget through. She had a bottle of water in one hand and her phone in the other, still tapping away with one thumb. She wasn't even looking at the screen! If there's ever a texting event at the Olympics, she'll win gold.

Naomi was next to her. 'What's up with you?' Naomi asked, carrying her lunch tray.

'We said your name a billion times,' Gidget said, nodding back to lunch queue. 'You totes ignored us.'

'I didn't mean to,' I said. 'I've just got a lot on my mind.'

'The robot?' Gidget asked.

'Wyatt?' Naomi said.

'Both,' I said.

Naomi could tell I was stressed and didn't want to talk about it, so she changed the subject. 'Biscuits and juice? Lunch of champions, right?'

I let out a small laugh. 'You're probably right, but when I want chocolate, I gotta get it.'

'Right?' Gidget said.

Naomi and I followed Gidget to a table.

'So…' Naomi said. 'What's bothering you?'

Naomi was the kind of friend who didn't pull punches. If she disagreed with you, she'd tell you. If she had a problem with something you were doing, she'd tell you. If you looked like life was beating you down, she'd ask how she could help you.

I really liked that about her.

'I'm not sure,' I sighed. 'Maybe it's Wyatt. Maybe it's the robot. Maybe it's Olivia tagging along everywhere.'

'Where's *everywhere*?' Naomi asked. 'She was only with us last night.'

I forgot that my friends didn't know I'd met with Wyatt earlier that morning. And I wanted to keep it that way... at least for a little longer.

'Yeah, that's what I meant,' I said. 'She's prob'ly gonna be everywhere now that Wyatt's on the team.'

Naomi narrowed her eyes. 'You're working with him on something else, aren't you?'

'No! I mean, yes!' I said, not sure which answer I was going to go with. And then

I surprised myself. 'Yeah, we're kind of checking out some things.'

'I think you're putting too much trust in Wyatt.'

'No, I'm keeping my distance. It's just that… I mean, he's kind of being cool right now, and there *are* things he can help with.'

'What're you guys up to?'

'I don't want to say anything yet. Not until I have a little more information.'

'More information on what? Have you forgotten that I used to be a Scavenger? That I know secrets about kids that would make their mothers weep?'

'No, I didn't forget.'

'Then tell me what you guys are doing. You need someone you can trust to keep you grounded.'

I said nothing.

'Whatever, dude,' Naomi smiled. 'I'll just have to be your secret guardian ninja then. I got your back from the shadows. I promise.'

141

'You don't have to—' I said.

'You can *trust* me,' Naomi cut in, making a serious face. 'I made my mistakes and I vowed never to make them again.'

'I know,' I said, finally reaching the table where the rest of Team Cooper was sitting. 'I need to get a little more info before I say anything else.'

I couldn't tell if Naomi was frustrated or hurt. 'Kay,' was all she said before taking the spot next to Gidget.

Zoe, Faith, Brayden and Slug were sitting quietly. Olivia was at the other end of the table next to Wyatt, who was in the middle of telling a story.

'... so I turned the amp off and got out of there as fast as I could!' Wyatt said.

Laughter exploded from the rest of the table. Wyatt's story must have been a funny one.

'What happened after that?' Brayden asked.

'They called my parents,' Wyatt said, 'but I never got in trouble for it. They figured I was a kid bein' a kid. I got a stern talkin' to from my parents because it *was* at a *funeral*, but I never got grounded or anything.'

'Man,' Slug said. 'My parents would *freak* if I ever did that.'

Wyatt chuckled, wiping a tear from his eye. And then he pointed at Brayden with both hands. 'Hey, dude, my dad said it was cool if we used his quad bike to go monster hunting sometime. He said it's fine as long as we don't ride after dark.'

Brayden slapped the table. '*Awesooooome!*'

Everyone was laughing at Wyatt's stories? Brayden and Wyatt had a monster-hunting date? What the heck was happening?

I dropped my biscuit on the table and sat on the other side of Naomi.

Wyatt went on with another story, making my friends laugh until their sides hurt. Zoe was in tears.

I wasn't sure what I was feeling. I *wanted* Wyatt to join the team. I *wanted* to give him another chance and I *wanted* my friends to make him feel welcome.

So why was it so weird?

Wyatt leaned back in his chair, and then did the two-handed point again, but this time at Slug. 'Hey, I'm makin' corndogs in the science lab tonight. How many should I put you down for? Two? Three?'

'Dude, five,' Slug said. 'And one pillow 'cause I'll be takin' a corndog nap afterwards.'

'You got it, brah,' Wyatt said and then looked at everyone else. 'Corndogs with a side of mac and cheese while we work! Sounds perfect!'

My friends nodded, talking about how much fun it was going to be.

Yep. Definitely weird.

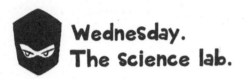 **Wednesday.
The science lab.**

I didn't see any other holiday ninjas for the rest of the day. And trust me, I was looking.

I was sitting in the science lab, waiting for the rest of my team to join me. It wasn't like any of them to be late, especially Zoe, but there I was... alone.

Carlyle's team was behind their sheet singing more pirate songs, swaying back and forth so hard that it felt like the floor was bouncing. How were they getting *any* work done? They spent all their time acting like a buncha dizzy pirates!

Every now and again, the sound of a hammer

clinking came from Carlyle's corner, but it wasn't from them working. It was in tune with the beat of one of their shanties.

Ugh! Stinkin' pirates!

A loud crash came from Dante's corner. I sat perfectly still, watching his shadow. He was kicking and pushing his robot, yelling because it wouldn't work.

'That kid…' I whispered. 'Just… wow.'

I heard Carlyle laugh loudly. I poked my head out from behind the bed sheet and looked at the pirate's section of the room.

Scattered across the floor were all the parts for their robot. One of the pirates was looking over the pieces. He looked like a confused dog, tilting his head.

Another pirate had a tricycle that he rode in small circles like he was part of a pirate circus or something.

At the edge of their circle was something that looked like an empty container. It was huge too. At least, huger than the robot my team was building.

And yeah, huger *is* a word. I just added it to the dictionary. Don't look though. It'll take time for it to update...

Carlyle's team hadn't even started building their robot!

The door to the science lab swung open, and Wyatt walked through. My entire team was behind him, listening to another one of his stories.

Olivia was the last through the door. She lagged way behind because of Brayden's cologne. Once she was in the room, she took the same seat against the wall, just out of noseshot of Brayden's musk.

'Right?' Wyatt said, flipping a chair around as

usual. 'If they didn't want kids crawling on the dinosaur fossils, they shoulda put a sign up!'

'Dude,' Slug said. 'You. Are. Wild!'

Wyatt laughed. 'You woulda done the same,' he said.

Zoe giggled like a schoolgirl with a crush.

Wyatt eyeballed me with a smile on his face. I couldn't tell if it was a villainous smile or not, but I couldn't shake the feeling that letting him on the team might've been a mistake.

'You guys are late,' I said, worried about the ton of work we still had to do.

Wyatt spoke for everyone. 'Sorry, man. Remember how I said I wanted to make corndogs? Well, the kitchen staff wouldn't let me bring a fryer in here, so I had to make 'em in the kitchen. We were eating.'

Slug leaned back, yawning. 'I'm stuffed.'

'You guys didn't invite me?' I said, my voice cracking slightly.

'Tried to find you, but couldn't,' Wyatt said.

'I would've texted you,' Gidget said. 'But I totes forgot.'

I didn't know what to say.

Slug snorted loudly as he slid to the floor. He was taking his corndog nap.

Wyatt got up from his seat, suddenly holding a knitted blanket. I had no idea where he got the blanket, but once again, I wasn't surprised. He placed it over Slug and said, 'Shhhhh, this little guy's pooped. Let him get some rest.'

Oh.

My.

Corndog.

Was I was still dreaming somehow? I pinched myself on the arm to find out.

Nope. Definitely not a dream.

Zoe and Faith were hard at work with the guts of the robot. It wasn't much, but Dr Tenderfoot said it didn't need to be. We only had a couple of days to finish the robot.

Zoe and Faith attached the battery pack to the stomach of the robot, which was then plugged into a small gearbox that was connected to the robot's shoulders.

Then the gearbox turned the main gear, which would move the robot's hand and make it look like it was waving. At the top of the robot was a light bulb.

Gidget and Faith took it a step further and connected a small metal shaft to the robot's side and wrist. The plan was that the main gear would turn and move two parts at the same time, pushing the arm up and waving simultaneously.

Pretty genius if you asked me.

Slug and Brayden were meant to be putting the finishing touches on the shell of the robot, to give it that extra boost of 'cool'.

Except the shell they made looked like a giant cow.

'What's that supposed to be?' Faith asked.

'A cow!' Brayden said proudly.

'Can't you tell?'

'Sorta,' Faith answered, walking slowly around the shell. 'I mean, it could be a cow from, like, a nightmare or something.'

Zoe perked up. 'Oh, nightmare cow! Gotta remember to tell Brody about that. It'd be a great band name.'

'It's not like I got much help from Slug,' Brayden continued, nudging the sleeping kid on the floor.

Slug snorted, but kept right on sleeping. His arms and legs twitched.

'Slug's chasing squirrels,' Gidget said.

'I think it looks great,' Naomi said.

'Thanks!' Brayden said.

'The competition's not based on appearances anyway,' Naomi added. 'So it's not like we'll lose points for having an ugly robot.'

Brayden made a face. 'Thanks?'

'Naomi's right, you guys,' Wyatt said. 'We just gotta make this thing work. That's all that matters.'

'Oh, it's *gonna* work,' Faith said confidently. 'Let's *do* this.'

Zoe looked at everyone with an excited smile. She placed her finger on the switch under the robot. 'Three ... two ... one ...'

Everyone held their breath. Zoe flipped the switch.

And nothing happened.

Zoe scrunched her nose and then flipped the switch back and forth rapidly.

The robot didn't do anything.

'C'mon,' Zoe said. 'Work!'

'We did everything right!' Faith said. 'It was working before we bolted it on!'

Wyatt leaned closer to the robot, inspecting the small battery pack. And then he pressed his finger on top.

Everyone jumped back as the robot sprung forwards, alive and moving the way Zoe and Faith had planned. The arm moved up and down while the hand spun in a circle, waving like it was a model in a robot parade. The light bulb at the top of the robot was shining brightly.

Zoe laughed, wiping sweat from her brow. She was more nervous than she let on.

'It was just a bad connection!' Wyatt said. He took his finger off the battery pack and the robot stopped moving. 'All we have to do is screw that part down a little tighter and it'll be good. We could prob'ly get away with just using a little tape.'

I sat back in my seat. 'Team Cooper's gonna

win this thing! That robot is flippin' sweet! I even like how it's gonna look like an ugly cow!'

'Hey!' Brayden said. 'It might be ugly on the outside, but she's beautiful on the inside!'

'That's all that counts,' Wyatt said. 'What should we name it?'

'Hup-Hup,' Faith said.

'I like it,' I said. 'Hup-Hup the robot.'

'We're gonna be rich!' Wyatt said. Apparently he still thought the prize was going to be a million dollars.

The whole team was excited.

Even Olivia was smiling from her chair. She had her phone out and was taking pictures of our robot.

We were almost totally finished, and we still had a whole day to go!

All the unease I felt about Wyatt disappeared as Hup-Hup came to life. Even Olivia sitting in the corner was fine with me.

Adding Wyatt to the team was a risk, but it turned out to be a good thing. He was making everyone laugh and work together. Maybe there was a reason he was always the leader of a ninja clan – *maybe* he was a good leader.

'Alright, guys,' Wyatt said. 'This calls for a *proper* celebration. Tonight. My house. Seven o'clock. Pizza is on me.'

'Boom!' Slug said, snapping to attention. 'Bring on the pizza! Wait ... what're we talkin' about? Where am I? Why do I taste corndogs?'

'Give him a minute,' Gidget said.

After a second, Slug stretched his arms out and drifted back to sleep.

'He'll be in and out for the rest of the day,' Gidget said. 'He'll wake up around midnight and complain about how he can't sleep. Then he'll play video games until about four or five in the morning. Then he'll sleep like a brick until it's time to go to school.'

'Livin' the dream,' Brayden said.

Wyatt pointed around the group. 'Alright, guys. I'll text you my address, and then I'll see you tonight. Cool?'

My friends, my *best* friends, all nodded. Wyatt went around the circle, adding everyone's number to his phone. My uneasy feeling came back as I watched him.

I couldn't put my finger on *why* it bothered me, but it did. Maybe it was my own problem. Maybe I was just being a little too suspicious when it wasn't necessary.

I shrugged it off as best as I could.

There were bigger things to think about, like getting our robot to actually work! Celebrating at Wyatt's house might be weird, but at least we were *celebrating*.

I was glad we weren't spending the rest of the night frustrated and kicking our robot the way Dante was probably going to do.

I looked at Dante's side of the room to see how he was holding up, but he was already gone.

 **Wednesday.
Wyatt's house.**

I had never been to Wyatt's house, but when I looked up the address on the internet, I found out that he lived only a couple kilometres away.

I know it sounds weird that I had no idea Wyatt lived so close to me, but I'll tell you why – his neighbourhood is *totally* different to mine.

His house … was a mansion. And his neighbours' houses? They were mansions too.

Brayden and I always rode by his street but the dirty looks the old people gave us were enough to keep us away.

There were times when life slapped me across

the forehead, and made me realise the world was much bigger than what I saw.

Let me put this in video game terms. When I go to the mall, the other shoppers are NPCs, non-playable characters. They don't affect my story, they're just doing their own thing in the background. I'll never see them again in my *whole* entire life. But to them? *I'm* the NPC.

What I'm trying to say is that seeing Wyatt's house made me realise he *wasn't* a non-playable character.

Nobody was. We were all on our own mission, passing other people who were on *their* own mission.

I know, right? I usually have to take a nap after my brain does that much work.

Team Cooper was at Wyatt's dinner table. Small pizzas lined the centre of the table. Each one had a couple of slices missing. It looked like a pizza buffet.

And it smelled amazing.

Everyone was in the middle of a weird conversation.

HEY... DOESN'T THIS PICTURE MAKE YOU HUNGRY FOR PIZZA?

WYATT'S HOUSE FOR PIZZA

'Whatever, dude,' Zoe said. 'You can believe what you want, but it's not possible.'

'It's *totes* possible!' Slug said defensively. 'Just 'cause you can't see it in your brain doesn't mean it *wasn't* happening!'

'You seriously believe that?' Zoe said. 'There's no way *literally everybody* was kung fu fighting.'

'Agree to disagree then,' Slug said, folding his arms.

Zoe shook her head, laughing.

An oven timer chirped from across the room.

'Gidget, this one's yours,' Wyatt said, pulling an oven mitt on. 'Spinach artichoke comin' right up.'

'Hey, Chase,' Zoe said. 'I had Wyatt make a buffalo chicken pizza for you. It's intensely spicy though.'

Buffalo chicken pizza was my new favourite thing. I always thought pizzas had to be just meat, cheese and pizza sauce until I tasted my first buffalo chicken pizza. It's chopped up chicken spread out across a layer of buffalo wing sauce and then blanketed with mozzarella cheese. And it is *awesome.*

Zoe set a slice on a plate and put it in front of the empty seat next to her.

Brayden leaned over the kitchen counter top, inspecting all the ingredients Wyatt had set out. 'Man, you're hardcore about cooking, huh?'

Wyatt smiled. 'My dad's a professional chef.'

'That's awesome,' Brayden said.

I took a huge honkin' bite of my buffalo chicken pizza. The crust was soft and kept warm by the piping hot buffalo wing sauce on top. The chicken was so tender that it almost melted in my mouth. And the cheese? I couldn't tell what was different about the cheese...

'You're tasting the blue cheese, aren't you?' Wyatt said, setting down Gidget's spinach artichoke special delivery on the table.

Pushing the food to the side of my mouth, I spoke. 'This is what blue cheese tastes like?'

'Yup!' Wyatt said, dusting the flour off his hands. 'Tastes like angel wings.'

'Chew with your mouth shut,' Zoe said, embarrassed for me.

'Oh my god,' Gidget sighed. 'I think I'm gonna *marry* this spinach artichoke pizza!'

Olivia was creating another pizza back by the ingredients bar. I was pretty used to her being around, but it was getting kind of weird that she didn't talk much. Brayden still smelled like a lumberjack, which was probably why she stayed at a distance.

I inhaled the rest of my slice and grabbed another.

There was even a mac and cheese pizza that Faith was guarding with her life. She didn't just take a slice of it either. She had the *entire* pizza in front of her, eating it with a fork. 'This,' she said seriously. 'This one's *mine.*'

Slug was awake, but it didn't look like he would be for long. On his plate were eight crusts – *just* the crusts. They were the only leftovers from his pizza-eating rampage.

Naomi only had one slice in front of her. It wasn't anything special either – just a slice of regular pepperoni.

Zoe leaned closer to me and spoke quietly. 'Wyatt's really turned over a new leaf, huh?'

I just nodded because I was chewing.

'What do you think?' she asked. 'Could this all be part of some larger scheme?'

I shrugged.

Zoe sighed. 'I hope this new version of him is for real.'

'It'd make life a lot easier, that's for sure,' I said after swallowing.

'For everyone,' Naomi added.

'He told me he wanted to be in our ninja clan,' Slug said.

'Nope,' I said. 'Being on our team is one thing, but I have to draw the line somewhere. We *used* to be in a ninja clan together. Didn't work out so well.'

Everyone devoured the rest of the pizza while joking and sharing crazy stories with each other. All in all, Wyatt's party turned out way cooler than I thought it would.

Wyatt brought out a bunch of board games. He set them on the table and said that Zoe would get to choose which one we played since she was the class president.

It was as if Wyatt had finally won everyone over.

Once I cleared my plate, I took it to the sink to rinse it off.

Wyatt followed me over. He leaned back, folded his arms, and spoke under his breath. 'So those pebbles… I figured it out.'

Olivia had taken the spot on the other side of me.

I glanced over my shoulder to make sure everyone was still at a distance. They were, but I turned the tap on so nobody would hear us talk. 'You know where the pebbles came from?'

Wyatt nodded. 'I had a hunch when we first found them, but I didn't wanna say nothin' until I knew for sure.'

'So?' I asked. 'Where?'

'The school roof,' Wyatt said.

'Those kids train on the roof?' I said, a little shocked.

'I doubt they're training,' Wyatt said. 'They'd make too much noise. They're probably just having meetings up there.'

'Actually,' Olivia said, 'the roof is solid enough that you probably wouldn't hear an elephant stomping around up there.'

'Well,' Wyatt said, 'there's really only one way to find out.'

'Find out what?' Naomi said, nudging me aside to put her plate into the sink.

'Um,' I said, hesitating. There wasn't any point in keeping Naomi or my other ninjas in the dark anymore. 'Wyatt thinks some new ninjas are meeting on the roof at Buchanan.'

'I *knew* it!' Naomi said with a scowl. 'I *knew* you two were doing ninja things behind everyone's back!'

'It wasn't *behind* everyone's back,' I said. 'I wanted to wait until we had more before coming to you guys.'

'You *always* say that,' Naomi said.

'So what's the game plan?' Wyatt asked me.

I answered Wyatt with another question. 'What happens if we find them there? It's not like we're going to do anything. I'm *not* fighting anyone because, one, it's stupid, and two, they outnumber us by a billion to two.'

'We can't do *nothing*,' Wyatt said.

'I know,' I said, frustrated.

'Let's just check it out,' Wyatt suggested. 'If they're there, we'll try to talk to them. If they're not, there's nothing to worry about.'

'Just talk to them?' Naomi said. 'About what? Life? Love? What we wanna be when we grow up?'

'Naomi's right,' I said. 'It's not like we can tell them to quit bein' ninjas.'

Wyatt clenched his teeth. 'Those kids can go play ninjas all they want somewhere else! Someone took my ninja clan, and I'm gonna take it back.'

'Babe,' Olivia said. 'Calm down.'

Wyatt took a breath. 'Look, those kids are up to something. You *know* it. We *all* know it! We just don't know *what* it is. And to be frank, I don't wanna know! I wanna stop it before it even happens!'

'Okay, *Frank*,' Naomi said, smiling.

Wyatt gave her a dirty look. 'I've missed you, Naomi,' he said sarcastically. 'You're a real breath of fresh air, but only if you're *into* breathing fresh air.'

Naomi and I looked at each other. Neither one of us could tell if that was a burn or not.

'Okay,' I said, finally. 'Let's meet tomorrow morning. Early. We'll check out the roof, but that's *all* we're gonna do. We're not gonna talk to them. They won't even know we're there.

The only reason we're doing this is to see if that's *actually* where they're meeting.'

Wyatt nodded. 'At least we're moving in the right direction.'

'I'll let the other guys know,' Naomi said.

'Really?' Wyatt snipped. 'Why do *they* need to know?'

'Because they're part of my ninja clan,' I said. 'And they're my friends. They're with us whether you like it or not.'

Wyatt pursed his lips. 'Fine,' he whispered.

 **Thursday.
The lobby.**

Brayden, Naomi, Gidget and Slug were filled in after Wyatt's party. I told them everything that happened with the red and green ninjas, and how Wyatt was booted from his ninja clan. I told them all about stealing my mask and how there was a new leader for each of those clans, but we didn't know who they were.

I even told them about the balloons in the Dungeon, and how they were fooled, thinking the black balloons were members of my ninja clan. Naomi laughed pretty hard at that.

'There's a bunch of those balloons on the

cafeteria stage too,' she said. 'I wondered what they were doing there. I guess they ordered too many.'

Once my ninjas were up to speed, they were pumped to help. They were waiting when I stepped through the front doors. Wyatt was there too, but Olivia wasn't with him.

'Sup, man?' Brayden said first.

'Stinkin' cold outside!' I said, rubbing my hands together.

'Normal people wear *winter* clothes during *winter*,' Gidget said, tapping on her phone. 'Hashtag frostbite. Hashtag not so smart. Hashtag actually pretty dumb.'

'I get it,' I said. 'I shoulda worn gloves.'

Wyatt was standing in front of the lift. The doors slid open immediately after he pushed the up arrow. 'Can we do this now? We're wasting time down here.'

All six of us got into the lift. We weren't stuffed into it, but there definitely wasn't room to do cartwheels. Well, even if there was only *one* kid, there wouldn't be room to do

"THE SCARIEST MOVIE I'VE EVER SEEN!" –SOME CRITIC

KIDS IN AN ELEVATOR

COMING SOON TO A THEATRE NEAR YOU... NOT REALLY.

cartwheels. Unless that kid was tiny. Like, *super* tiny. Like, fifteen-centimetres-tall tiny. How cool would that be? They could ride all kinds of remote controlled cars and helicopters and— Y'know what? Never mind.

Gidget bobbed her head back and forth to the beat of the lift music. Even Slug kind of bounced up and down, dancing. He had a small bag of chocolate drops in his hand that he shook like a tambourine.

Once the lift reached the second floor, the doors slid open. Wyatt was the first one out.

'This thing doesn't go straight to the roof?' I asked.

'No,' Wyatt said, coldly. It was different from how he had acted all week. 'But there's a couple of other ways to the roof.'

'If it's a ladder, then count me out,' Gidget said. 'I'm not really in a ladder-climbing mood today.'

'Baby,' Wyatt said.

Gidget glared at Wyatt. Then she held her hand out at him. 'Whatever, dude. Talk to the hand.'

'Hey, 1990 called,' Wyatt said. 'They want their insult back.'

'Oh yeah?' Gidget fumed. 'Well, 2060 called. They said you died and nobody went to your funeral!'

Everyone gasped.

Gidget shook her head. 'Nope, nope, nope. Too dark. I knew it was too dark the second it left my mouth.'

'Anyways ... there *is* a ladder, but there's also a staircase,' Wyatt said, pulling open a large metal door that led to the stairwell. Again, Wyatt was the first to go through. He was a dude on a mission.

'Wait up, dude!' I said, catching up to Wyatt on the stairs by skipping every other step. 'We're just seeing if they're there! That's it!'

Wyatt stopped on the step in front of the door to the roof. 'Of course,' he said. 'I'll be as quiet as a kitten.'

And then Wyatt kicked the door open.

'A really *loud* kitten,' he said as the door slammed open.

And right there, on the school roof, was a herd of holiday ninjas. Kids in red and green ninja robes clumped together in groups, talking. *Not* training. And I think some of them even had cups of coffee. Were we interrupting an evil ninja business meeting?

'Gimme back my ninja clan!' Wyatt shouted as he stepped through the door.

I should've let him deal with the ninjas by

himself, but I just couldn't. I grabbed his arm
and pulled him back into the stairwell. The
door swung shut on its own, leaving us in quiet
darkness.

'So much for staying hidden,' Naomi said at
the back of the group.

'Does this mean we go back down, or ...'
Slug said, trailing off. He threw a couple more
pieces of chocolate into his mouth.

'Are you crazy?' I said to Wyatt.

'It was *my* clan,' Wyatt growled. 'And I want it back!'

'You know that you might not get it back, right?' I said. 'That was always a possibility!'

'Uh, guys?' Gidget said coolly. 'We should prob'ly get goin' now, huh? I mean, there *is* an army of ninjas right outside the door, and they know we're here.'

'Maybe they'll go away,' Brayden said.

'Really?' Gidget replied. 'You think if we turn the lights off, they'll think nobody's home?'

'Maybe!' Brayden said, panicked.

The doorknob jiggled. I grabbed it and pulled as hard as I could, keeping the door shut.

'Just let go!' Wyatt said.

'You got some sorta death wish?' I said. 'If I let go, this stairwell gets *flooded* with ninjas, and if that happens, we're toast! Lightly buttered toast!'

'Dudes, real quick,' Slug said. 'Are chocolate drops supposed to make your mouth burn?'

I'm not sure Slug's mind was completely aware of the situation.

'No,' Gidget said to her brother. 'They're not.'

'Man,' Slug said, tilting his head. 'I should prob'ly get to the nurse then.'

'How are we so different?' Gidget sighed.

'Um, helloooo?' I sang. 'We're kind of having a crisis up here!'

'Oh, right,' Slug said. 'Holiday ninjas.'

'Get back down the stairs,' I said to my ninja clan. 'I'll hold the door as long as I can, but it ain't gonna be long!'

Since Naomi was the last in line, she ran to the bottom of the stairs so the others could go down too. I knew she would've stayed if she could.

Gidget snapped a quick selfie with me in the background. I might've been two seconds away from death, but I still made a dorky face. After that, she and Slug hopped to the bottom of the stairs.

Brayden didn't budge. 'I'm not leaving,' he said boldly.

'I know,' I said.

The door opened about a crack. Brayden

174

grabbed my forearms and helped me pull it shut. The ninjas on the other side were shouting and pounding on the metal door.

'So what now?' Wyatt asked. 'We're just gonna sit here, pullin' the door shut all day long?'

Wyatt was right. At some point, we were gonna have to let go.

'Okay, okay, okay,' I said quickly. 'On the count of three, we make a break for it.'

'Back down the stairs?' Wyatt asked.

'No, through the door,' I said sarcastically. 'Yes, down the stairs!'

'You don't need to be like that,' Wyatt huffed.

'This is all your fault!' I said. 'Kicking the door open was never part of the plan!'

'Not *your* plan,' Wyatt said.

'We were supposed to work together on this!'

'And we are!' Wyatt said. 'I'm sorry if I have a habit of working faster than you. That's how I get things done, Chase!'

'Children, please,' Brayden said. 'Can we act like grown-up kids and focus on what's happening right now?'

The door inched open again. Brayden and I pulled it back shut.

'There are so many ninjas out there that I can't even see the roof!' Brayden said.

And then Wyatt's angry eyes disappeared. 'Okay,' he said. 'Kicking the door might've been a mistake.'

'Ya think?' I said.

'On three?' he asked me.

I nodded and took a deep breath. 'One…'

Brayden stared into space, waiting.

'Two…'

Wyatt was also staring at nothing.

'… *three!*'

All three of us spun around to run down the stairs, but the second I let go of the doorknob, it swung open. All at once, the ninjas on the other side spilled into the stairwell, rolling over one another like a landslide of ninjas.

'Watch out!' Wyatt squealed in a super high-pitched voice as he disappeared into the mess of tumbling ninjas.

Brayden reached his hand out to me, but it

NINJA LANDSLIDE!

was too late. We both were sucked into the mass of holiday ninjas. The only thing we could do was ride the wave until we hit the bottom of the stairs.

I didn't know where Naomi, Gidget and Slug were, but I was glad they managed to get away.

When the world stopped spinning, I found myself on top of a pile of red and green ninjas. They were groaning in pain. My body hurt too, but there wasn't any time for me to rub my sore spots.

I grabbed Brayden's arm and pulled him out.

Wyatt was at the door that led to the hallway, holding it open. 'C'mon!' he said. 'Before they get up!'

Back at the door to the rooftop, someone shouted, 'They're getting away! After them!'

The ninjas on the ground heard the order, but they didn't move. They were still nursing their bruised knees and elbows.

Brayden and I wasted no time and dashed through the door Wyatt was holding open.

There were a few kids in the hallway, staring in our direction. It was a good thing too – the ninjas wouldn't come after us since there were witnesses.

Naomi, Gidget and Slug were nowhere to be seen.

'Be cool,' Wyatt said.

I tried to straighten up, but it hurt. I hunched over slightly, keeping a hand on my lower back. Pretty sure I looked like my grandpa.

Brayden was limping next to me. Wyatt put a hand on his shoulder to help him keep balanced, even though Wyatt was trying to walk through a limp of his own.

We all stared at each other for a moment.

And then, because of how redonkulous we looked, we started laughing.

'You should be a singer for an '80s band with a scream like that,' I said to Wyatt.

Wyatt rolled his eyes and faked a laugh. 'Bwah ha ha, very funny. My voice gets high when I get excited.'

The clock on the wall said we only had a few minutes until school started. We agreed to meet again during lunch.

Waiting wasn't going to be the hard part. The hard part was going to be figuring out what to do next.

 **Thursday.
Lunch.**

My ninja clan was on the top step of the nook in the lobby. I could see them through the tinted windows that lined one side of the cafeteria. After scarfing down my lunch, I dumped my tray and stepped into the lobby.

Wyatt was sitting with them talking about what happened after they escaped the stairwell. He even pulled his shirt up to show them the bruise he got from tumbling down the stairs.

'Seriously, dude,' Gidget said, disgusted. 'Put your shirt down.'

Olivia stepped out of the cafeteria after I did,

walking towards the group. But when she got closer, she started sneezing. She sat on a bench and wiped her nose.

'Stop using that cheap perfume!' she yelled at Brayden from across the lobby.

'It's cologne,' Brayden yelled back. 'And it was super expensive!'

'It was a waste of money because you smell like a pinecone!' Olivia said.

'*I smell like a man!*' Brayden shouted.

I SMELL LIKE A MAN!

Naomi and Gidget giggled. Slug smiled, shaking his head. Wyatt was sitting with his back against the wall, staring angrily at nothing.

I waved my hand in front of Wyatt's face. 'You figure anything out since this morning?'

'No,' he said, shaking his head. 'I still don't know who the leaders of the ninja clans are.'

Glancing at the front office, I said, 'We could always go to the principal with this. Tell him that a bunch of ninjas are training on the roof and...I'm just now realising how crazy it all sounds when I say it out loud.'

'Right?' Brayden said. '*We'll* be the ones locked away in detention.'

'Doesn't matter,' Naomi said. 'Those ninjas aren't on the roof anymore. They probably cleared out right after we got away.'

'Could we challenge them?' I suggested.

Wyatt sat up. 'I thought you didn't fight.'

'No, not to a fight,' I said. 'To, like, a dance off or— Never mind. I knew that answer was dumb before I finished the sentence. What's wrong with me today?'

'How about we do nothing?' Naomi said.

'I *like* that idea!' I said.

'Seriously though,' she said. 'For all we know, those ninjas could just be a buncha kids that want to hang out and practise ninja moves. Maybe there *isn't* some kind of ultimate plan they're working on. What if all this running around and chasing they're doing is *because* you guys keep messing with them?'

Naomi had a point. The only times I ran into them that week was because *I* was the one going after them.

The first time was on Monday when I helped Wyatt.

The second time was when I used myself as bait.

And the third time was earlier that morning when we barged in on them drinking coffee.

All three times, it was *me* going to them.

'I think we should leave them alone,' Naomi said. 'I bet this is just some kind of little club for them. If that's all it is, then we're fine.'

'*I'm* not fine,' Wyatt said. 'It's *my* club to lead! Not *theirs*!'

Naomi looked right at Wyatt. 'Bummer, man.'

Wyatt's jaw flexed, but he didn't say anything. He stood up, and then he walked away down the hall. Olivia ran to catch up with him.

Wyatt definitely wasn't happy. What did he think was going to happen though? That he was going to get his red ninjas back just like that? There *had* to be a part of him that knew it might not happen, right?

**Thursday.
After school.**

Everyone on the team was in the science lab after school. Everyone except Wyatt. I hoped he was just running late.

Slug and Brayden had finished the outer shell and were letting the paint dry before putting it on Hup-Hup, our robot.

Zoe and Faith were switching Hup-Hup on and off, amazed that the machine was working perfectly.

Carlyle's team was quiet for a change. Wanna know why? They weren't even there.

I peeked over the sheet to get a glimpse of

their robot. I was shocked to see that all the pieces from Tenderfoot Industries were still spread out on the floor in messy piles. I wasn't sure Carlyle's team even *had* a robot.

Dante was in his corner. He was sitting on a chair, gawking at the broken robot that he trashed the day before. 'How could I have done this...' he whispered to himself.

'That's the face of a kid who can't even anymore,' Naomi said when she saw me staring at Dante.

'Can't even what?' I said.

'You know,' Naomi said. 'He is *unable* to even. He's *lost* the ability to even. *He can't even!*'

'Someday I'm gonna make a poster that says "you *can* even",' I said.

'Where's Wyatt?' Zoe asked, finally realising the last member of our team was absent.

'Probably blowing off steam somewhere,' I said. 'Punching tree trunks or something.'

Faith raised her eyebrows. 'Is he mad?'

'He's not happy,' I said.

'What happened?' Zoe asked, concerned.

'Did you guys get in a fight? I *knew* he was trouble!'

'No,' I said. 'Nothing like that. He's just going through some things. He probably wants to be alone.'

'I did,' Wyatt's voice came from the door. He was leaning against the frame with his hands in his pockets. 'I'm better now though.'

'Oh, good,' Zoe said. 'You're a member of our team, and I'd hate for you to miss out on anything.'

'Where's Olivia?' Brayden asked.

'She had to take off or something,' Wyatt said. 'Her dad was going to pick her up today. Never mind her though. I wanted … to … um …'

Everyone fell silent as Wyatt stumbled over words like they were speed bumps.

'I know that I … it's not been the greatest … um …' He stopped, taking a deep breath. Finally, he said, 'I'm sorry I was kind of a jerk today.'

Whoa. Was Wyatt apologising to *me*? He was looking right at me. There was the word 'sorry' in his sentence, and it *wasn't* followed by a 'but…'.

Yup. I think Wyatt was apologising. It was slow and awkward, like nails on a chalkboard. I just wanted it to be over already!

'It's cool,' I said, nodding.

'What did you do?' Zoe asked, confused.

'I don't really wanna talk about it,' Wyatt said. 'Chase was right. He's been right the whole time. And I'm just saying sorry.'

I think Faith's mind was blown because her jaw dropped and her eyes were wide.

'Y'know,' Zoe said, 'when Chase let you on the team, I wasn't happy about it. I don't think any of us were. But you proved us wrong. Especially with all the snacks.'

Wyatt's eyes softened. 'Then I guess it was a good thing I ordered some cupcakes for our final day working as a team.'

'There's a lot more happening at school this year,' Zoe said. 'Maybe we'll all be on the same team again.'

'That'd be awesome,' Wyatt said, glancing

at his watch. 'The cupcakes'll be here any second.'

'It's time for our break anyways,' Zoe said, standing up. 'Are they delivering them to the lobby?'

Wyatt nodded.

'Cool,' Zoe said. 'Faith and I will go grab them. Anyone else wanna come too?'

'Totes,' Brayden said, standing. 'We'll have to wait outside though because the doors are locked after school finishes. Someone will have to let us back in, so one of us has to stay in the lobby.'

'I'll stay in the lobby,' I said. I didn't feel like standing outside in the cold.

'Me too,' Wyatt said.

Wyatt and I were sitting on the top step in the nook, watching through the window as the rest of our team jumped off the benches outside.

Naomi wasn't with them. She forgot something at her locker and headed that way.

Without warning, Wyatt jumped to his feet, staring down the hall.

I didn't have to ask what he saw because I knew the look on his face. I'd worn that look at least a hundred times before.

There were ninjas in the hallway, and they were coming for us.

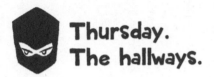 **Thursday.
The hallways.**

The cupcakes Wyatt ordered hadn't been delivered yet, so the rest of Team Cooper would be outside for another few minutes. That was good. It meant they weren't in danger when the holiday ninjas stormed the halls.

The front office was empty. And then I realised that it wasn't that the teachers were gone at the worst times — it was that the ninjas waited *until* they were gone.

Wyatt walked towards the middle of the lobby. 'I can hear their footsteps.'

'That means they *want* you to hear their footsteps,' I said.

'If *I* were still their leader, it would mean that,' Wyatt said, 'but since I'm *not* their leader, it means they're terrible ninjas.'

Pulling my mask over my face, I said, 'You should get your mask out.'

'I don't *have* a mask,' Wyatt growled. 'Remember? They *took* it from me.'

'You don't have extras?'

'Uh, yeah, I had a *hundred* extras,' Wyatt said. 'I gave them to the kids in my clan before I got booted!'

The footsteps were getting louder, and they were coming from the hallways on both sides of the lobby.

'They're gonna corner us out here,' Wyatt said.

'There's no way they'd try to fight us, right?' I asked, unsure. 'I mean, we're two guys against their what? Hundred ninjas?'

'It's probably not that many,' Wyatt said. 'Trust me, I know. Trying to get that many

192

ninjas to work together on *one* thing is impossible.'

'Okay, so *less* than a hundred, but more than two,' I said. 'Ugh…sounds like a story problem.' I paused, and then chuckled. 'One ninja clan leaves their dojo travelling at ten kilometres an hour. A second ninja clans leaves *their* dojo going fifteen kilometres hour. How long will it take for the second ninja clan to pass the first one?'

Wyatt sighed, watching the hallway. 'They're leaving two *different* dojos. It doesn't work. What if the dojos were on opposite ends of the planet? Then the second ninja clan would *never* pass the first one.'

'I, uh…' I said, racking my brain. 'Never mind. It was just a joke.'

'Get your head in the game, Cooper,' Wyatt said. 'We gotta act fast. Those ninjas are gonna turn the corner any second!'

'We can't go outside,' I said. 'And both hallways are out, so—'

'Too late!' Wyatt said, pointing at a group of kids running straight for the lobby.

I spun around to check the hall behind me. Kids had already turned the corner there too. My stomach lurched, but I quickly realised the students weren't wearing ninja outfits. They were wearing gym clothes.

I tore my mask off and stuffed it back into my hood before anyone could see me wearing it.

Relieved, I watched the two groups of kids run past each other in the lobby. It was the track team. Sometimes they ran laps in the hallways when it was too cold to run outside.

'Comin' through, guys!' the track team captain called out.

Wyatt swallowed hard and let out a sigh. He looked at me as the track team passed us on both sides. The crowd was thick enough that it was hard to see the walls behind them.

'Maybe we're being a little paranoid,' Wyatt said to me.

The track team started to thin out, and after a couple of seconds, they were gone. Wyatt and I watched them disappear down the hallway.

'That was a little freaky,' I said.

'Not as freaky as us,' a girl said from behind Wyatt.

Wyatt and I turned around, and I almost jumped out of my skin.

There, facing the two of us, was a small pack of green ninjas.

Wyatt and I turned around to run, but the ninjas were too quick. They circled around us, blocking our path. The only way out was the door to the cafeteria.

I ran for it – I wasn't about to be in the

UGH... THEY'RE EVEN POSING.

middle of a ninja mosh pit. Wyatt followed me,
pushing me through the door.

For the second time that week, Wyatt and I
fell through a door. We rolled to a stop on the
cold floor of the cafeteria. Lunch tables had
been folded in half and set up in a long line
down the back of the lunchroom. The huge
fluorescent lamps that hung from the ceiling
were switched off.

The sun was still out, but the tinted windows
meant it was dark in the cafeteria. It looked
like it was the middle of the night.

'Get off me,' Wyatt groaned.

'Sorry,' I said, getting to my feet.

The green ninjas stepped through the door calmly. They knew Wyatt and I had nowhere to run, so they weren't in any hurry.

And then a single red ninja appeared behind them. He was wearing a yellow cape over one shoulder. I had seen him once before, but not for more than a couple of seconds.

'What do you want?' Wyatt said. 'Not enough that you guys took my mask, huh?'

'*I* didn't take your mask,' the girl ninja said. The rest of the green ninjas stood behind her with their arms folded. She must've been their new leader.

The red ninja in the back said nothing.

'Then what do you want?' Wyatt said loudly, but not shouting.

'We're here to deliver a message,' she said.

'And what's that?' Wyatt asked, clenching his fists.

The ninja took a moment to answer, eyeballing Wyatt. 'Give up,' she finally said. 'We *know* you've been looking for us all week. Stop it now, or else.'

'Or else?' I repeated, kind of surprised. 'A threat? Really?'

The ninja's eyes darted to me, but she didn't answer.

'I'm not giving up until I get my ninja clan back!' Wyatt said, pointing at the red ninja in the back. 'You messed with the wrong kid, pal!'

'What makes you think you'll get it back?' the green ninja leader asked. 'Your ninjas have *abandoned* you.'

'Then I won't stop until *every* ninja clan at this school is *destroyed*,' Wyatt said.

The green ninjas didn't like that. They stomped across the cafeteria with eyes on fire.

The red ninja stood perfectly still, like he was only there to watch the action.

Wyatt dashed forward to meet the green ninjas head on.

The whole thing had got out of hand. Wyatt and I were about to get our butts handed to us on a silver platter, and why? Because I had to stick my nose where it didn't belong! I had nothing to do with Wyatt and his red ninja clan! I shouldn't have even been there!

At that moment, a door at the back of the cafeteria slammed open so hard that it shook the floor. The green ninjas stopped. So did Wyatt.

I *might've* yelped like a frightened baby deer. I don't know. There was so much happening that it was hard to tell. Maybe there *was* a frightened baby deer somewhere in the cafeteria. How could someone even know there *wasn't*? Here – *prove* to me that there *wasn't* a frightened baby deer in there. See? You can't.

All I could make out were shadows of other ninjas pouring out of the door that had opened at the back of the room. There were dozens of them. Literally, dozens!

And they were all wearing black. Chalk dust poured from the door, masking them slightly. They looked like floating ninja ghosts.

'What the heck?' the green ninja leader whispered.

The black ninjas stopped just inside the cafeteria. They stood like statues and said nothing, which was scarier than it sounds.

The green ninja leader stepped backwards as her ninjas did the same. She didn't say anything.

I squinted at the black ninjas, trying to see who they were. My ninja clan only had five members in it – Brayden, Gidget, Slug, Naomi and me – but these kids were wearing my ninja clan's colour.

So who were they?

And then I saw her. It was just a glimpse, but that was all it took for me to understand immediately.

Naomi was hiding in the door where all the ninjas had come from. She winked at me.

Naomi had made good on her promise. She was my secret guardian ninja.

When I squinted, I could see that the heads of the ninjas were the black balloons I had told her about earlier in the week. She had painted eyes on them. Their bodies looked like black rubbish bags.

Naomi had made an army of fake ninjas.

Puffs of chalk dust burst around the green ninjas, and they began to disappear one by one, scared of being outnumbered. Although the illusion was kind of shattered because I could see them running away after throwing their little chalk pouch on the floor. Ninja vanish? More like ninja hobble away.

The two holiday ninja leaders were the last in the cafeteria. They were staring across the room at the fake army.

And then the worst possible thing that could happen, happened.

One of the black balloons popped.

The green ninja shrieked. '*His head exploded!*
His head ex—wait a second...'

The green ninja turned around to command
her other ninjas to attack, but they were gone.
The red ninja grabbed her elbow when she tried
to run back to us.

'No!' the red ninja growled. 'There's no time
for this! They won't listen, so we'll *make* them
pay!'

'That's such a *bad guy* thing to say!' I said.

'Have fun explaining to the rest of Team
Cooper how Hup-Hup was crushed,' the red
ninja said.

'*Hup-Hup the robot?*' My heart sunk. 'You
wouldn't...'

But the two ninjas were already out the door
and sprinting towards the stairs.

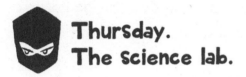

Thursday.
The science lab.

Wyatt and I ran as fast as we could but the ninja leaders were too fast. They took the stairs, like, four at a time!

The rest of my team was still outside waiting for the cupcake delivery. I was bummed that they were out there because if they were inside, I knew they would've kept Hup-Hup safe.

Instead, Hup-Hup was alone and unguarded.

When we got to the top of the stairs, the two ninjas had just turned the corner.

'We're not gonna catch them in time!' Wyatt said.

'We can't just stop!' I said, feeling my side cramp up.

I took the corner too fast and slammed into the wall. The science lab was only a few doors down, and it was open. The two ninjas were already inside.

Wyatt passed me, slowing down as he got to the door. I pushed through the pain and caught up with him.

We were just in time... to watch the red ninja dropkick our robot, sending parts flying in all directions.

I dropped to my knees. *'Noooooooooo!'*

'You're just a poser!' Wyatt shouted. He was just as upset about our robot as I was. 'Just some *kid* pretending to be the leader of my ninja clan! If you're gonna steal my clan out from under me, don't hide behind your mask! Show me your face, you coward!'

The red ninja stood up straight, and then he did exactly as Wyatt asked. He took off his mask.

Wyatt's knees almost gave out, but he

managed to keep himself up. I choked out a gasp.

It was Carlyle, the pirate. Wyatt's cousin.

CARLYLE
...THE PIRATE.

...ew.

↖ NOT SURE HOW HIS CAPE IS BLOWING IN THE WIND.

Carlyle's yellow cape swished out, and I saw that it wasn't *just* a cape. It was a pirate flag with a picture of a skull.

Wyatt's face grew red with anger. He didn't seem as surprised as I was.

'Figures it was you,' he said calmly. 'Can't get any kids into your little pirate club, so you just take *my* ninja clan instead. Weak, dude. Weak.'

'Ye lost control of yer crew long ago, mate!' Carlyle said.

'Why are you still talking like that?' I said as I got to my feet. 'Are you a pirate or a ninja?'

'I be a *ninja pirate*, ye pox-faced kraken!' Carlyle said, squeezing one eye shut.

'That's not even a thing!' I said.

'It is now, ye parrot-lovin' sea bass,' Carlyle said.

I put my hands up. 'Ugh, enough with the pirate insults. I get it.'

Wyatt stepped forward. 'I didn't lose control of *anything*, you backstabber. You *took* my ninjas from me! And then you made them steal my mask!'

'Aye,' Carlyle said. 'You were lame as a leader, cousin. There was so much more ye coulda done with yer ninjas, but ye never did.'

'Like sell a bunch of t-shirts?' Wyatt said.

Carlyle laughed. 'D'ye really think this has got to do with merchandise, cousin?'

In that moment of awkward silence, my brain connected the dots.

'You're jealous,' I said to Carlyle. 'That's what this is, isn't it? Wyatt's ninja clan is bigger than your pirate crew, and now you're taking what he's built.'

'Keep yer mouth shut,' Carlyle said.

'You snuck your way into my ninja clan,' Wyatt said, catching on. 'And staged a mutiny against me...'

'Yer only now realising that?' Carlyle said.

'Yes!' Wyatt shouted.

I watched them shout it out at each other. The pirates at Buchanan School had grown weak. Instead of building them back up, Carlyle took the red ninjas. Wyatt was bound to find out sooner or later, and being Wyatt, he wasn't going to take it well.

The whole thing had gone from a simple ninja clan takeover to something *much* bigger...

A battle between two cousins.

And somehow, I had got stuck in the middle of it.

Whoops.

And then, believe it or not, things got even *more* twisted up …

'Yer at yer wits end, cousin. Give yerself up, and I'll keep ye from walkin' the plank,' Carlyle said.

'Walk *what* plank?' Wyatt huffed. 'You know what, you're such a poser that I'm not even *surprised* it was you this whole time!'

'No?' Carlyle said. 'How's this for a surprise?'

The green ninja leader untied their mask, and pulled it off their head.

It was Olivia.

OLIVIA! LEADER OF THE GREEN NINJAS!

Wyatt actually *was* shocked this time. His bottom lip quivered. 'Babe…?'

'I was gonna break up with ya,' Olivia said. 'But then ya went and got yourself on Chase's team.'

'Made it too easy to spy on yer robot,' Carlyle said.

At that moment, Team Cooper stepped through the doors behind us. They stopped, staring at the bizarre scene that was in front of them. Naomi was the only one from the team who wasn't there.

I couldn't even imagine how it looked to Zoe. There we were, Wyatt and I, standing over our destroyed robot. Carlyle and Olivia wearing ninja costumes and no masks.

A cloud of chalk dust burst around Carlyle and Olivia, and they were gone. I had no idea how they left the room because the only way out was through the door that Team Cooper was standing in.

Zoe stared at the pieces of the robot we all worked so hard to build.

The rest of my friends looked like life had just slapped them across the face.

Zoe glared at me. '*What did you do?*'

'I didn't do anything!' I said defensively. 'You saw who did it!'

'No!' Zoe shouted. 'This is all because of you and your little ninja game! You *killed* our project with this stupid secret you have! You've gone too far this time!'

'But I—'

'*Neh!*' Zoe snipped. It was her way of making me keep my mouth shut. 'I know what I saw. I saw you and Wyatt and Carlyle and Olivia, but you know what? I don't blame them! I blame *you*! If you didn't run around the school pretending to be a ninja, we'd still have a shot at winning tomorrow! You *know* how important this is to me! You *know* Dr Tenderfoot is a big deal to me!'

I opened my mouth to speak, but Zoe shut me down with another '*Neh!*'

'You vouched for Wyatt!' Zoe said.

Team Cooper nodded from behind Zoe.

'And Wyatt vouched for Olivia!' Zoe said. 'Okay, so Olivia and Carlyle are working together? Too bad she was hanging out on *our* side of the room all week!'

'She was a spy,' I said under my breath.

'What normal kid can say that seriously?' Zoe said. 'I know I can't! I can't go around talking about ninjas and pirates and spies without sounding absolutely ridiculous!'

Zoe's chest was heaving up and down.

'And *you*,' she said, looking at Wyatt. 'Of course Carlyle did this! Of course Olivia did this! Of course you're the one behind it all! I guess we're all just paying the price for trusting someone we *shouldn't* have!'

Wyatt started to talk, but Slug cut him off.

'Dude,' Slug said. 'Was this your plan the whole time?'

'Yeah,' Faith added. 'Were you playing us?'

'Of course he was! It's so obvi!' Brayden said.

Wyatt didn't bother saying anything else. He pushed his way through the team and walked out the door.

And then the rest of my team left the room, one after the other, in total silence, until I was alone.

Everything happened so fast that I was still in shock. Leaning my back against the wall, I slid down until I was sitting on the floor. In just twenty short minutes, everything had gone from absolutely great to absolutely awful.

The broken parts of Hup-Hup were spread across the floor in front of me.

I'd made mistakes and messed things up in the past, but this time felt different. It felt worse.

Much, much worse.

Thursday.
The school parking lot.

I was in a funk. I could barely even bring myself to clean up the mess that Carlyle made when he booted Hup-Hup across the room. My phone buzzed in my front pocket. I pulled it out and read the message. It was from Zoe.

my dads gonna be here any minute

She sounded mad, that's for sure.

Bits of Hup-Hup were still scattered across the floor, but I was beat. Cleaning could wait until tomorrow morning.

I grabbed my book bag, pulled one of the

straps over my shoulder, and headed down to the lobby.

The rest of Team Cooper was already gone. Zoe was alone on a bench outside, staring into space. She was slouching, which was weird for her. She always nagged me about my poor posture.

The air felt colder than normal. It bit at my cheeks the second I stepped outside.

I didn't say anything when I sat next to her.

She sighed. But not the kind of sigh that was like, '*Look at me.*' She was sad.

'Zoe,' I finally said. 'I'm *really* sorry.'

She took a deep breath. 'I know,' she said.

'No,' I said. 'I mean, I'm really, *really* sorry.'

Zoe looked at me. 'I know you are,' she said. 'But it's just a robot. There are worse things happening in the world.'

'But it's a big deal to you,' I said. 'I know I let you down with, y'know … my *ninja* stuff.'

'Why do you still do it?' Zoe asked. 'Why do you play that game?'

Zoe knew it was more than a game to me.

'If you didn't do any of that,' Zoe continued, 'you wouldn't have any problems.'

'I don't know why I do it,' I said, but the truth was I knew exactly why.

There were a lot of bad eggs at this school, and if there wasn't someone there to keep them in line, the balance would shift in their favour. *I* had to be that someone.

But I couldn't tell Zoe that.

'I know I shouldn't have trusted Wyatt,' I said.

Zoe tilted her head back and groaned. 'I can't believe I'm about to say this but...While I was waiting, I saw Wyatt leave through one of the side doors. He didn't look happy, like, at all. His face kept twitching. It looked like he was really beating himself up about Hup-Hup.'

'Really...' I said.

Zoe nodded. 'Mmhmm. If he was in on it, then why wasn't he with Carlyle or Olivia? He had the look of a boy who had been burned by his best friends. I really don't think Wyatt is to blame this time.'

I was mad at Wyatt, but I felt the same way that Zoe did.

Yes, he was one of the bad eggs. Yes, he'd been a rusty nail stuck in my big toe since the first week of school. And yes, his plans were always cranked to eleven on the evil-villain scale.

But Wyatt wasn't the one who destroyed our robot. That was Carlyle and Olivia.

If I really wanted to be fair to Wyatt, I had to admit he was *probably* innocent, no matter his past.

Zoe's dad pulled into the parking lot.

'I'll figure out how to make this right,' I said.

Zoe smiled. 'I know you will,' she said. 'You always do.'

With less than a day until the competition, I had no idea how I could fix any of the mess I had created.

To be honest, it was starting to look like my life would be a lot easier if I just gave up and let Carlyle's team win.

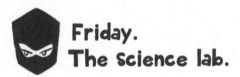

Friday.
The science lab.

I was heading for the science lab when I noticed that the door was propped open. Someone had got there before me, which wasn't a big surprise since it *was* the day of the robot competition.

What was surprising was that it was Wyatt.

He sat on a backwards chair the way he always did. On the floor in front of him were the shattered parts of our robot, spread out like he was trying to figure out how to put it back together.

When he saw me, he nodded.

'What're you doing?' I asked.

'What's it look like?' Wyatt said.

'It looks like you're trying to fix the robot.'

'Because *that's* what I'm doing.'

I didn't know what to say. Should I have brought up Carlyle? Olivia?

'What do you think?' I asked, taking the seat next to his. 'Is Hup-Hup done for?'

Wyatt shrugged. 'I don't even know where to start. I had to set it out like this so I could see what it's *supposed* to look like, but all I see are random parts.'

'Let's just sweep it into the bin then,' I said. 'We'll clean it up and throw in the towel.'

'No!' Wyatt said angrily. 'I will *not* let Carlyle steamroll right through me.'

'I think he already did,' I said.

'Dude,' Wyatt said, sitting up. 'I'm not gonna roll over and die like that. Carlyle, my *cousin*, burned me. Olivia, my *girlfriend*, burned me. My ninjas … *burned* me. I've got no one, but I'm *not* defeated and I'm not giving up.'

I had watched Team Cooper put the robot together all week, and the way Wyatt set everything out made it easy for me to figure out how to put Hup-Hup back together.

I knelt down and started putting the pieces back in their place. Wyatt helped when he could, but it was mostly pointing at parts and asking if I needed them.

Even though Carlyle had kicked our robot, the damage wasn't as bad as I thought. Most of the parts clicked back into their spot. Sure, it might've been an ugly version of what it used to be, but at least it wasn't a shattered mess anymore.

Wyatt and I looked back and forth between Hup-Hup and the *many* extra parts we had left over.

'Those things were in the first version of the robot?' Wyatt asked.

'Yeah,' I said. 'But not this version. Hope they weren't important.'

'Guess we'll find out,' Wyatt said.

Pushing all the spare parts aside, I reached

under the robot and flipped the switch to turn it on.

Hup-Hup didn't move. Something buzzed quietly, but the light bulb on top didn't even flicker.

'C'mon, man,' I said, flipping the switch back and forth.

'Maybe those extra parts *were* important,' Wyatt said, glancing at the pile of parts.

'What'd you do that first day it didn't work?' I asked, looking at the battery pack.

'Oh, the battery wasn't connecting properly,' Wyatt said. 'I just made sure it connected. Push the battery down hard. If that's the problem again, it should fix it.'

I took Wyatt's advice and pushed against the battery. I held my thumb in place and switched it on again, but nothing happened except for the quiet buzz.

I followed the wires from the battery pack to the small motor at the shoulder, and then studied the gears to see if something was just stuck.

Finally, I admitted, 'I have no idea what I'm looking at.'

'Step aside, rookie,' Wyatt said. He stared at the machine for a moment before saying, 'Yeah, I got nothing.'

'The problem's probably with your wires,' someone said from behind one of the hanging sheets.

Wyatt and I looked at each other, surprised.

'Uh, hello?' I said.

'Hi,' the voice replied.

'Um, how long have you been there?'

'The whole time.'

'You didn't hear anything we—'

'I heard every word you said. Carlyle, Olivia, ninjas.'

'It's Dante,' Wyatt mouthed.

Dante peeked out from behind his sheet. 'I don't care about any of that.'

Wyatt and I weren't sure what to say.

Dante pointed at Hup-Hup. 'If it's not your battery pack, it's probably your wires. I heard it buzzing, so it's *trying* to work.'

'Ummmm,' I said, pinching the plastic-coated wires between my fingers. They felt a little loose, but I really didn't know how they were supposed to feel.

Dante could tell. 'Look where the wires hook into the gearbox at the top,' he said. 'What's it look like?'

Following the wires with my fingers, I found the spot Dante was talking about. The plastic on each of the wires was peeled back, probably from when Carlyle booted it. The thin copper wires underneath were shredded, barely making contact with the gearbox.

'They're about to fall off,' I said, turning to where Dante's voice had come from, but he was already hovering over my shoulder.

'See that?' Dante said, pointing at the frayed end of the wires. 'The robot's buzzing because there's some power, but it's not getting enough to work properly. All ya gotta do is...' Dante trailed off as he pinched the frayed wires. He rolled his fingers back and forth to get the wires to stay in place. 'Try it now.'

I flipped the switch. Hup-Hup jumped to life, raising its arm while its hand spun in circles. The light from the bulb was so bright it almost blinded me.

'Nice!' I said, excited.

It was ugly and sloppily put back together, but our robot was working again.

'Thanks, dude,' I said, looking back at Dante's side of the room. 'You know what you're doing with this stuff, so ... what happened over there with *your* robot?'

Dante pressed his lips to the side. 'Robotics is kind of a hobby for me. I love working on stuff like this, but... I get frustrated when things don't work. I mean, I was already frustrated 'cause nobody wanted to be on my team, but y'know, whatever, I guess.'

I felt bad for him as he walked back to his corner of the science lab.

'There are a ton of things robots can do,' Dante said. 'I was trying to make mine do too much.'

'Bummer,' Wyatt said in a way that sounded like he didn't care.

'No biggie,' Dante said. 'Good luck with your robot. You only have Carlyle to worry about. I completely trashed my robot so I'm out.'

Hup-Hup kept waving, like it was saying goodbye to Dante. The hairs on my arm stood on end. Dante helped fix our robot, which meant we *didn't* have to sit back and let Carlyle win. There was still a chance. School didn't start for another twenty minutes. With that much time, I could grab some breakfast in the cafeteria ... or I could keep working on Hup-Hup.

'Dante!' I called out.

He spun around. 'Yeah?'

'What *else* could you do with this thing?' I asked.

Dante smiled. He started rattling off a list of little things we could add to the gears to make the robot do even more.

While Dante was talking, Wyatt leaned closer to me. 'We *have* our team,' he whispered.

I looked Wyatt in the eye. 'Be like water, bro.'

The muscles in Wyatt's jaw twitched. He wasn't happy with it, but he didn't have a choice. I was the team leader. And Dante was now on Team Cooper.

 **Friday.**
The library.

Dante and I carried Hup-Hup down the stairs carefully. We had covered it with one of the sheets so nobody could see it before the competition.

Wyatt went to the library to make sure we had a spot up the front. But I reckon he just didn't feel like helping. He wasn't happy that Dante was part of the team, but I didn't care. Dante had been having problems all week, and I don't even know why it took me *that* long to come up with the idea of him joining Team Cooper. All this junk with the red and green ninjas had been more of a distraction than I thought.

Carlyle and his team never showed up to the science lab, but I snuck a peek at their section of the room. It had been completely cleaned out as if they were never there.

Their robot was probably gonna blow ours away. I knew it, especially after Carlyle destroyed ours. But staying in the competition wasn't about winning anymore. It was about showing Carlyle that we weren't going to sit back and let him do whatever he wanted.

But as Dante and I carried Hup-Hup down the hall, I had a glimmer of hope in the back of my mind that *maybe* we had a chance at winning.

I sent a text to my friends before going to the library, letting them know that I had a surprise and that I hoped they showed up.

Principal Davis held the library door open so Dante and I could carry our robot through.

The crowd of kids parted as we walked through. The library was just as packed as it had been on Monday. Dr Tenderfoot wasn't anywhere I could see.

When we got to our spot in front of the staircase at the centre of the room, I thought we'd have a table to set Hup-Hup down on, but we didn't. Instead, the middle of the room was taped off and empty. It looked like a boxing ring.

Carlyle's team was in one corner, huddled around their robot, which was also covered with a sheet. Carlyle was in the middle of the huddle, but Olivia wasn't with him.

Wyatt was waiting in the opposite corner all by himself. Zoe and the rest of the team weren't there. Without them, things felt foggy, like I was watching my life from behind a dirty window.

'About time,' Wyatt said. 'What took you so long?'

'What took us so long was that there were only two of us carrying this beast,' I said. 'We woulda been here sooner if you helped.'

'You coulda just asked,' Wyatt said.

'I *did*!' I said.

Wyatt pushed his hands into his front pockets. 'Didn't hear ya.'

'Right,' I said.

Dante and I carefully set Hup-Hup on the floor and pushed it gently into the ring.

I looked over my shoulder, and checked my phone for texts. Nothing.

'Have you seen the others yet?' I asked Wyatt.

He shook his head. 'Nope,' he said. 'But I sent them a text about how they didn't need to show up.'

'*You did what?*' I said. 'Dude, what's the matter with you?!'

'What?' Wyatt said. 'They don't need to be here! They didn't help fix our robot, did they? It was just you and me!'

'And me,' Dante said.

Wyatt ignored him. 'Why should they stand with us when *we* were the ones who did all the work?'

I couldn't believe what I was hearing. Was Wyatt actually delusional?

'We *didn't* do all the work,' I said. 'We *all*

worked on it, and then because of *you*, it was destroyed!'

'And then you and I fixed it,' Wyatt said, nodding like we were on the same page.

'And me,' Dante added.

Again, Wyatt ignored him. 'Dude, what's the big deal? That means this bombastic prize will be just for us. What d'you think it'll be? A million bucks? How sweet would that be?'

'I don't want that!' I said.

Wyatt looked at me like I was crazy. 'You ... *don't* want a million bucks?'

'No, of course I want a million bucks,' I said. 'But I don't want to shut out the rest of the team!'

'Chase, listen,' Wyatt said. 'You're not thinking of the bigger picture. Think of yourself for once, dude. Your chums will be mad, but they'll get over it.'

'Not the point,' Zoe said from behind us.

Team Cooper was with her – Brayden, Faith, Gidget, Slug and Naomi. And they looked angry.

'Cripes,' Wyatt said. 'I told you guys you didn't need to be here!'

Zoe laughed loudly. 'Where do you think we were gonna go?' she asked. 'This is a school-wide event! And I'm the *president* who *planned* it!'

'Did you think we'd just stay home or something?' Faith asked, pushing past Wyatt. She lifted a corner of the sheet covering our robot. 'Is this Hup-Hup? Did you really fix it?'

'Uh, yeah,' Wyatt said. '*Chase* and *I* fixed it.'

'With my help,' Dante added sheepishly.

Wyatt tried to ignore him again by talking, but I shut him down right away.

'Oh, Dante's on our team now,' I said. 'He was the one who helped us fix it. Without him, Hup-Hup would still be dead.'

I expected them to kick up a fuss, but they didn't.

'Cool,' Slug said, putting his hand on Dante's shoulder. 'But if you're on our team, you're gonna have to work on your anger management, okay?'

Dante laughed.

'Nobody cares that Dante's on the team now?' Wyatt asked, clearly annoyed.

Everyone shook their heads. Brayden sprayed a shot of cologne on his chest.

'What?' he said as everyone stared at him. 'In case we win! I wanna smell good for the ladies!'

The lights in the library switched off and then back on again, letting everyone know the competition was going to start in a minute.

'Have you seen Dr Tenderfoot yet?' Zoe asked, looking over everyone's head.

'No,' I said. 'He's supposed to be here, right?'

'I think he was here before school,' Zoe said. 'But I never got a chance to see him.'

'Maybe his helicopter hasn't dropped him off in the parking lot yet,' Brayden said.

'He came by helicopter?' Naomi said. 'Man, how cool is that?'

'Super cool,' Dr Tenderfoot said, walking past us towards the staircase. 'But definitely *too* cool for this guy. I drove.'

Dr Tenderfoot was wearing his top hat, tuxedo jacket, jeans and sneakers. A small chain dangled from the monocle on his right eye.

Tenderfoot took a few steps up the staircase and grabbed the microphone.

'Welcome, welcome, children of Buchanan School! It's been entirely too long since we last met, and I hope life has been good to you in the meantime.'

A couple of kids clapped, but stopped when they realised nobody else was.

'As you know, we have three teams that will be participating in the competition,' Tenderfoot continued. He pulled his sleeve up and glanced at his watch. 'Which we really must begin as quickly as possible because I've got a load of meetings today.'

'See?' Zoe said. 'He's a busy dude.'

'Remember,' Dr Tenderfoot said. 'The winner today will receive a prize bigger than they can even imagine.'

'A million bucks split nine ways is still a ton of money,' Wyatt said, hopeful.

'Who said it was a million bucks?' Gidget said, perking up. 'Is that really what's on the table?'

'No,' Zoe said. 'Nobody knows what the prize is. Wyatt's just hoping, that's all.'

'First up,' Dr Tenderfoot continued loudly, pointing one finger in the air. 'Dante Sullivan and his team, if you could please make your way to the ring.'

Dante stepped forward with his hands stuffed into his pockets. 'I'm sorry,' Dante said, embarrassed. 'But I don't—'

I jumped forward, waving at Dr Tenderfoot. 'He's on our team now!' I said, cutting Dante off. 'We thought we could do more if we teamed up!'

Dr Tenderfoot's eyes squinted at me like he was studying some kind of bug. He took his monocle in his fingers and adjusted it. And then he pinched his moustache and rolled the end into a point.

'Interesting,' Tenderfoot said. 'So rather than three teams competing, we'll only have two?'

'Yes, sir,' I said.

Dr Tenderfoot said nothing. He just stared at the centre of the ring while twisting the end of his moustache. The microphone was picking up the breaths he took through his nostrils.

'What's he doing?' I asked.

'Thinking?' Zoe said. 'I don't know.'

Finally, the man with the moustache jolted back to reality. 'Very well! The competition will be between *two* teams. I believe it makes things a little more interesting. We'll have a clear winner and a clear loser. The stakes are high, are they not?'

All he got was confused murmuring from the crowd.

'Our first robot will come from Chance Cooper's team,' Dr Tenderfoot said.

'Uh,' I said, raising my hand. 'It's *Chase*. *Chase* Cooper.'

'Of course,' Dr Tenderfoot said, nodding once at me. 'My sincerest apologies, Chase Cooper.'

'It's cool,' I said, pushing our robot out to the centre of the ring. 'People make that mistake all the time.'

Except they really didn't. I just didn't want Dr Tenderfoot to feel stupid. I pushed Hup-Hup to the centre of the ring and hesitated, holding a corner of the sheet. I'm not sure why I paused. Maybe it was because I knew our robot looked like junk after putting it back together. Or maybe it was because those moments before a big reveal were my favourite.

I always got chills at the movie theatre right before the show started. When the previews end and the lights dim? Man, that's one of the best feelings in the world. It makes my heart race. Sometimes it's better than the movie!

I pulled the sheet off Hup-Hup, showing it to the entire school. Wyatt, Dante and I managed to force the cow shell over the top of it, so it kind of looked okay, but if I told you a bunch of kindergarteners built it, you'd totes believe me.

Gidget snapped a selfie with Hup-Hup. Brayden and Slug gasped, shocked. Zoe and Faith raised their eyebrows at the same time. Naomi let out a puff of air through her nose with a short laugh.

Dante was smiling like the robot was his BFF. Wyatt just looked angry.

Some kids in the crowd giggled. I ignored the few comments that said the robot looked pathetic.

'Dr Tenderfoot,' I said boldly. 'This is Hup-Hup. It's our robot, and we're proud of it. It might not be pretty, but it's *ours*.'

Dr Tenderfoot's face was hard to read. He didn't look at the robot like it was a pile of junk. He looked at it like he was seriously interested.

'Go on,' he said. 'Explain your choice in design.'

I looked at Carlyle, and then back to Tenderfoot.

'We had some trouble about halfway through the project,' I said, shooting a quick look at

Carlyle. I wasn't going to rat him out. 'This little guy's had a hard life for only being a week old.'

'Doesn't matter,' Tenderfoot said, half smiling. 'What matters is that it performs the way you've built it to.'

Nervously, I dropped to a knee and pressed on the switch on the bottom of the robot. The last time we tested it, Hup-Hup worked perfectly, including the change that Dante made at the last second.

I looked at the rest of my team, who were watching with shiny eyes. I took a deep breath, and slid the switch to the 'on' position.

Nothing happened.

I stared at the robot, hoping I could *wish* it to life. Did robots have fairy godmothers? Pshhhh, who am I kidding? *Of course* robots had fairy godmothers!

'Don't do this to me, Hup-Hup,' I whispered, barely loud enough for even me to hear. 'Don't embarrass me in front of my friends!'

I flipped the switch, but again, nothing.

Wyatt was standing in the corner, clenching his fists.

Dante looked like he was about to cry. I think he wanted the robot to work more than I did.

And then I heard the quiet buzzing sound. The frayed wires! I put my hand through the hole and rolled the top of the wire between my fingers the same way that Dante had.

Just like that, Hup-Hup jumped back to life.

Its little robot arm raised and lowered perfectly. Its hand twisted in circles to look like it was waving at everyone in the library. And with Dante's addition, Hup-Hup slowly tilted back and forth while its body rotated.

Dante had a thin plastic pipe that pushed against the ground every time the hand rotated. Because the pipe was attached at an angle, it made the robot slowly spin in a circle.

The light bulb made the robot's eyes shine bright, and for a moment, I felt like it was a living thing.

Our team cheered loudly, raising their arms

HUP-HUP♪
...don't make fun, please.

in victory — not because we thought we were going to win, but because we got the dang thing to work at all!

Dante was celebrating the hardest. He was running back and forth, giving awkward high-fives to anyone who wanted one.

'Disqualified!' Carlyle shouted from his corner. 'Their robot didn't even work at first! It wasn't finished in time! That prize should be ours!'

Dr Tenderfoot raised his hand to tell Carlyle to quiet down. 'It's alright,' he said calmly. 'All that matters is that it's doing what it was built to do. Some bumps in the road are inevitable, and can be a learning experience in and of themselves.'

Carlyle stepped back, but didn't say anything else.

Dr Tenderfoot extended his hands towards my team and applauded. Everyone in the library followed his lead.

'Next team?' he said, waving at Carlyle.

Carlyle put his hand on his chin and cracked his neck. The library was so quiet that you could hear the crunching sound.

He tapped once on the top of his covered robot, which by the way, was the size of a baby bear. The machine jostled, and then started moving towards the centre of the ring all by itself!

'Interesting,' Tenderfoot whispered, his voice carried by the microphone.

'Avast, ye landlubbers!' Carlyle said as he walked with his robot. 'Pay close attention – history is about to be made!'

'Dude,' Brayden said. 'That thing's moving by itself!'

Carlyle's covered robot stopped at the centre of the ring and spun in a circle.

'Allow me t'introduce ye to my team's 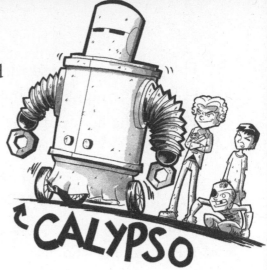 project, Calypso!' He pulled the sheet off the machine they had been working on all week.

It was amazing. The last time I saw their robot, it was a pile of pieces on the floor, and that was on Wednesday! In less than two days, they had created a mechanical masterpiece.

It looked like it was from a sci-fi movie. It had a body with two arms and a head. Instead of legs, it had a metallic cover that I think was hiding wheels. Little lights blinked all over the robot's head.

Calypso wobbled back and forth, making its way around the ring. As the robot circled around, it waved at the kids in the library.

The gears inside squeaked as they moved.

Everyone was quiet, staring in awe.

'How in the heck did they build that thing?' Naomi said.

'They're good, I guess,' I said.

Carlyle walked proudly with his hands behind his back as he spoke. 'Calypso is a state-of-the-art robot, who also obeys voice commands. Calypso, stop!'

The robot stopped in place, turning its head towards Carlyle.

'Calypso, bring me my book bag!' Carlyle commanded.

The little lights blipped on the robot's head, and then with a very mechanical voice, it said, *'As you wish, master.'*

'Voice activated *and* can talk?' Brayden said. 'Dude, we lose. That's it. Game over. We're all outta lives and outta continues.'

Dante frowned.

The whole library watched as Calypso wobbled over to Carlyle's bag, picked it up by the straps, and then wobbled it back to the pirate. When Calypso finished its mission, it swung back to face the crowd.

Everybody cheered. I even clapped. It was seriously impressive.

'Calypso,' Brayden said. 'Come here and give me a high five!'

The robot turned and said, '*Unknown user. Command not recognised.*'

Brayden laughed, along with a bunch of other kids in the crowd.

Calypso turned towards Carlyle, as if it was waiting for the pirate to tell it what to do. Carlyle squinted, and then waved his fingers slightly, signalling to the robot that he approved the high five.

The robot shook its head slowly.

'Whoa,' I said under my breath. 'That thing just refused to obey a command! This is it... this thing is the beginning of the robot apocalypse!'

Zoe must've heard me because she rolled her eyes. '*Nerd.*'

Carlyle stomped his foot down and stuck out

his chest. 'Calypso,' he said sternly. 'High five the student who asked for it!'

Calypso hesitated, but finally wobbled over to Brayden. He held his open hand out.

'What if that thing high fives your hand right off?' I joked. 'It *is* a robot, it probably doesn't know its own strength!'

Brayden looked at me, panicked. Just as Calypso swung its robot arm towards his \hand, Brayden pulled it back and the robot missed.

Brayden's pine-scented cologne wafted in the air around me. Calypso stumbled forward. I could hear the robot whisper, *'Seriously?'*

It was weird that a robot would have the ability to feel frustration.

And then Calypso sneezed. *'Aaa-choo!'*

Even Dr Tenderfoot raised an eyebrow.

'Whoa,' Slug said. 'Any robot that sneezes is too real for me.'

'Wait a second,' I said, watching the robot as it wobbled back to Carlyle. I turned to Brayden. 'Gimme your perfume!'

Brayden pulled the small bottle from his book bag. 'It's *cologne.*'

'Whatever!' I said, taking the bottle. I raised the cologne and pointed it at Calypso, but the robot was too far away.

Without thinking, I ran towards the robot, spraying the cologne as I circled around it.

'*What're you doing?*' Carlyle shouted.

'Young man!' Dr Tenderfoot boomed from the staircase. 'This rude interruption will cost you the competition! You will be disqualified if you don't exit the ring!'

Even Principal Davis shouted at me from the edge of the library. 'Chase, get over here, right now! This is extremely inappropriate!'

Kids were booing, yelling about what a sore loser I was.

But all the shouts stopped when Calypso sneezed again. '*Aaa-choo!*'

All heads turned towards Carlyle's robot.

Finally, I stopped. Through the fog of pine scented cologne, I watched as Calypso tried to wobble away from the manly musk of lumberjacks.

But the robot couldn't move fast enough. The cloud of cologne drifted slowly around it. And then the sneezing fit started. Over and over, Calypso sneezed. And each sneeze grew stronger than the last.

'No!' Carlyle said. 'You can't get my robot wet! That's cheating! She'll short circuit! I mean, *it'll* short circuit!'

With a final, super strong sneeze, Calypso doubled over, sending its head flying through the ring. It rolled to a stop at the bottom of the staircase.

Dr Tenderfoot stared at the robot's head on the floor in front of him. When he looked back at Calypso, he pressed his lips to one side of his face and shook his head slowly.

Calypso was still in the ring. The robot's body was intact, blinking with colourful lights.

On top of the
robot's shoulders
was another head,
but it wasn't a robot.

It was Olivia. Olivia
dressed in a robot
costume.

Slug gasped.
'Olivia's been
turned into a machine!'

Gidget sighed heavily, shaking her head. 'It's
a costume, dude… How are we even related?'

Slug's eyebrows furrowed a bit as he breathed
through his mouth. 'Oh, that makes more sense.'

Olivia sat in the centre of the ring, shocked.
But her frown flipped into a smile because what
else can you do when you get caught cheating?
And then she sneezed one final time. It was
strong enough that she tipped over and fell to
the ground.

The rest of the robot costume peeled apart.
Olivia had been moving the robot using the
tricycle I had seen in the science lab.

Dr Tenderfoot didn't waste a second with accusations or speeches about cheating and disappointment. He pointed at Hup-Hup, and announced, 'We have our winner, ladies and gentlemen!'

'Why couldn't you hold your sneezes back?' Carlyle said angrily.

Olivia was rolling around on the floor, stuck in her robot costume. 'Because I'm human! He sprayed that garbage all over and made me sneeze like crazy! Gag! So gross!'

'Well, thanks to your dumb allergies, we lost!' Carlyle said.

'Don't you dare blame me for this!' Olivia said. 'This was *your* idea! And because of that, we're out a million bucks!'

'A million dollars?' Dr Tenderfoot said into the mic. 'There's no way that ridiculous costume cost a million dollars to make.'

Carlyle glared at the man with the moustache. 'No, ye scurvy-infested fool! The million-dollar prize for the winner of the competition!'

The crowd fell silent.

'Scurvy-infested fool?' Dr Tenderfoot repeated.

'Oh, snap!' Slug whispered. 'Carlyle's finished!'

'Whoops,' Carlyle said.

Tenderfoot didn't say anything else to Carlyle after that. He just waved his hand at Principal Davis, who understood immediately that he was supposed to remove the pirate from the room.

Olivia wiggled around to free herself from her costume. It took nearly a minute and everyone watched in awkward silence.

Finally, she managed to get it off. She was still sneezing every few seconds. Then she looked at Wyatt with soft eyes. 'Hey, babe! Looks like we won, huh?'

Wyatt scrunched his nose, shocked that Olivia was trying to switch sides again. Principal Davis shouted for her to get to the library doors.

A bunch of students covered their mouths and said, '*Ohhhhhhhhhh!*'

Dr Tenderfoot continued quickly. 'Would the leader of the *real* winning team please come to the staircase?'

Zoe patted my back, nudging me forward. It was a little embarrassing, but in a good way.

But as I started for the staircase, Wyatt grabbed my elbow, pulling me back. He peeled out past me, running at full speed until he got to Dr Tenderfoot's side, halfway up the stairs.

'What's he...' I said.

Wyatt pointed his fingers at the crowd, and then grabbed the microphone from Dr Tenderfoot, but not without a small struggle from the man with a moustache.

Naomi stood next to me, and together we watched as Wyatt did his usual 'Wyatt' thing.

'Thank you!' he said into the microphone. 'Thank you so very much! It's been a long journey, but I did it! With the help of my team, of course! But it was mostly me, the team captain! So here I am, ready to claim the prize on behalf of my team!'

'Oh, really?' Dr Tenderfoot asked.

'Yup,' Wyatt said. 'Lay that million bucks on me, Dr Tenderbutt. I'm ready to be so rich that I can literally *buy* happiness!'

Dr Tenderfoot looked confused. 'Who said *anything* about a million dollars?'

'Uhhhh,' Wyatt said. 'It's *not* a million bucks? That's fine. Whatever the prize is, I'll go ahead and take it now. It's still a prize greater than I can imagine!'

'It is, young man,' Dr Tenderfoot said. 'The prize is…'

Tenderfoot paused for effect. All the kids in the library fell silent, waiting for him to drop the bomb.

Even Wyatt was staring, slack-jawed. His eyes grew wider with every nanosecond that passed.

'Victory,' Dr Tenderfoot said with a calm voice.

Wyatt dropped the mic, but it was so quiet that everyone could still hear his voice. 'Victory?'

'*Victory* is its own reward,' Tenderfoot said, pinching the end of his moustache.

'That's nothing,' Wyatt said. 'That's not something greater than I can imagine! Something greater than I can imagine would be a trip to Saturn! It'd be my own island in the Bahamas! *It'd be a million bucks!'*

'Whoa,' I said, blown away – but seriously, not at all bothered by what Dr Tenderfoot had said.

'The machine your team built won the competition,' Dr Tenderfoot explained. 'You may not think much of it, but look at the other two teams…one cheated, and one completely disappeared. Only *your* robot remains in the ring. This competition *wasn't* as easy as everyone thought it would be, was it?'

Wyatt didn't answer.

'So the reward for the winning team,' Dr Tenderfoot said again, 'is *victory*. You've overcome great hurdles to get here. Imagine what else you could do.'

'Laaaaame,' Wyatt sang, but he wasn't one to miss an opportunity to gloat. He put his hands in the air and waved victoriously.

The applause from the crowd was slow and awkward at first, but eventually grew into a mighty roar that sounded like it was going to bring down the house. Kids will cheer for anything if enough people are cheering with them.

And Wyatt ate it up. He put his hands together over his head and pumped them up and down. *This* was his reward. *This* was his victory.

Naomi nudged me with her elbow. 'You can stop this, you know. *You're* the team captain. It should be *you* up there.'

'I know,' I said, watching Wyatt. 'I don't care.'

'I didn't think you would,' Naomi smiled.

Everyone was cheering loud enough that nobody could hear our conversation.

'Just because Carlyle and Olivia were busted doesn't mean the red and green ninjas are finished,' I explained. 'They'll be back, and I think I'm going to need Wyatt's help. If I go up there and call him out, he'll just get angry. Besides, look at him. I think he needs this more than I do.'

Naomi watched Wyatt overdo it on the

staircase. He had started flexing his arms and posing like a body builder.

I knew I wasn't going to get in the middle of a family feud between Wyatt and Carlyle, but I couldn't be sure *they* would keep me out of it.

'But you're letting him get away with a lie,' Naomi said.

'Nah, I don't see it like that,' I said. 'We couldn't have built Hup-Hup without Wyatt's help. It doesn't make a difference whether it's him or me up there. And as the *actual* team leader, I'm okay with him taking credit. It's not a battle worth fighting. And right now, with what Carlyle's done, I think we'll need as many people on our side as we can get. I have this awful feeling that a war is coming.'

'So you're cool with all this?' Naomi asked me. 'You're forgiving him?'

I thought about it for a second. 'Yeah,' I said without a doubt. 'Isn't that the risk you take whenever you forgive anyone? Either they've changed, or they'll burn you again.'

'I suppose,' Naomi said. 'It's never as black

and white as that though. I don't even think this is about Wyatt, is it?'

I couldn't help but smile. 'If I *didn't* let him on our team, I'd be on the path to the dark side.'

'Nerd,' Naomi rolled her eyes. '*Such* a nerd.'

I laughed and Naomi slugged me in the arm. Great. Now *Naomi* was in on it too.

Wyatt was still on the staircase handing out high fives like he invented them. Dr Tenderfoot wasn't next to him anymore.

In fact, he was next to me.

'Impressive work, Chase Cooper,' Dr Tenderfoot said.

'Thanks,' I said, and then waved to the rest of my friends behind me. 'But I couldn't have done it without my team.'

'Well, they had a good leader,' Tenderfoot said. The monocle on his eye reflected the library lights.

I bit my lip, glancing at Wyatt.

'I'm not talking about that showboat,' Dr Tenderfoot said. 'I'm talking about you.'

I was speechless, even though my mouth was trying to say something.

'Don't make a thing of it, young man,' Dr Tenderfoot said. 'That's what makes you, *you*. You don't need all the…' He waved his hands at Wyatt and made an annoyed face. '*Show*.'

'Thanks,' I said. Then I remembered the blank slips of paper from the beginning of the week. 'Hey, about the names you picked out of your hat…'

'What about them?' Tenderfoot's moustache twitched.

'All the slips of paper were blank,' I said.

Dr Tenderfoot took his monocle between his fingers and let it dangle in front of my face. My reflection was wonky on the lens.

I took it carefully, not wanting to break it.

Dr Tenderfoot took a slip of paper from his tuxedo pocket, holding it up to me. It was white. Completely blank.

'Look through the glass, m'boy,' Dr Tenderfoot said with a hint of excitement in his voice.

I brought the monocle to my eye and looked at the slip of paper he was holding. It wasn't blank anymore. It was a list of meetings.

'It's, like, invisible ink or something?' I asked, my jaw dropping.

'Something like that,' Dr Tenderfoot said. 'Because, well... why not? Invisible ink is fun, isn't it?'

For the first time, I wasn't intimidated by Dr Tenderfoot. He might've been a genius inventor, but he was still a kid at heart.

I looked down at the monocle. It was a lot heavier than I would've guessed.

When I looked up to give it back... Dr Tenderfoot was gone.

He was rushing for the library doors.

'Wait,' I shouted.

'Keep it!' he said over his shoulder. 'I got a million of them!'

'Huh,' I said, inspecting the monocle once more before stuffing it into my front pocket.

My friends surrounded me, almost tackling me to the ground. Everyone was there – Zoe, Faith, Gidget, Slug, Brayden, Naomi and Dante. They were excited, celebrating our win, even though there was no prize.

We spent the rest of the morning playing with Hup-Hup and showing everyone how we made it work.

Wyatt was still taking all the credit, but it didn't bother me.

Was he still the bad guy? Maybe. Maybe not. I think he was stuck somewhere in the middle. I wasn't sure what his endgame was, but I knew it was *something*. And with Wyatt's history, it was something *big*.

But we had a deal. We'd leave each other alone after the holiday ninjas had been dealt with. I could only hope he'd keep up his end of the bargain.

Plus, with the threat of ninjas in the shadows, I'd rather have Wyatt where I could see him, and there in the library, the entire school could see him.

And no matter how shady he was, he still helped the team build Hup-Hup.

It wasn't much, but it was a start.

Melvin, one of the school reporters, held up a camera and my team huddled around me. 'Yearbook photo on three! One…two…'

'Chase,' Naomi said from the end of the group.

I looked to see what she wanted, but she didn't say anything. She was making an ugly face at me.

Without thinking, I made my best ugly face back at her.

Naomi smiled as her head snapped back towards the camera, which flashed.

Sighing, I rolled my head back because I knew exactly what happened. Naomi just proved her point and the yearbook was going to have evidence of it.

Ugly faces *were* contagious.

Diary of a 6th Grade Ninja Series

Collect the SET!

Marcus Emerson 5
Diary of a
6th Grade
NINJA
Terror at
the Talent
Show

Marcus Emerson 6
Diary of a
6th Grade
NINJA
Buchanan
Bandits

Marcus Emerson 7
Diary of a
6th Grade
NINJA
Scavengers

Marcus Emerson 8
Diary of a
6th Grade
NINJA
Spirit
Week
Shenanigans

Marcus Emerson 9
Diary of a
6th Grade
NINJA
Scavengers
Strike Back

Marcus Emerson 10
Diary of a
6th Grade
NINJA
My Worst
Frenemy

Marcus Emerson is the author of several highly imaginative children's books, including the 6th Grade Ninja series, the Secret Agent 6th Grader series, *Lunchroom Wars* and the Adventure Club series. His goal is to create children's books that are engaging, funny, and inspirational for kids of all ages – even the adults who secretly never grew up.

Marcus Emerson is currently having the time of his life with his beautiful wife and their amazing children. He still dreams of becoming an astronaut someday and walking on Mars.

BONUS FACT ABOUT THIS BOOK:
THIS IS A PICTURE OF MY SON, PARKER, AND ME. CHASE'S FUNNY FACE IS BASED ON THIS FUNNY FACE THAT PARKER MAKES. HE DOES THIS IN EVERY PICTURE BECAUSE HE KNOWS IT MAKES PEOPLE LAUGH. EVERY. SINGLE. PICTURE.